Lords, Ladies, Butlers and Maids

Period Erotica in Private Houses

T0318071

mischief

This novel is entirely a work of fiction.
The names, characters and incidents portrayed in it are
the work of the author's imagination. Any resemblance to
actual persons, living or dead, events or localities is
entirely coincidental.

Mischief
An imprint of HarperCollins*Publishers*
77–85 Fulham Palace Road,
Hammersmith, London W6 8JB

www.mischiefbooks.com

A Paperback Original 2013

First published in Great Britain in ebook format by
HarperCollins*Publishers* 2012

A catalogue record for this book is
available from the British Library

ISBN-13: 9780007553471

Find out more about HarperCollins and the environment at
www.harpercollins.co.uk/green

Contents

Contents

Lips Like Heaven
Donna George Storey

A good servant is invisible. To be seen is to ask for trouble.

So my aunt told me before I went into service, soon after my parents died.

But she hadn't warned me not to be heard.

My 'trouble' began innocently enough, with all four members of the staff gathered around the piano in the drawing room, enjoying a bit of music after a hard day's work. Had the family been in residence, we would have properly confined ourselves to the servants' hall, but the stylish London townhouse looked more like a storeroom as we prepared the newlywed home of Mr and Mrs Charles E. Shaw. Each day more crates arrived, luxurious furnishings ordered by the master's wife-to-be. Meanwhile Alice and I polished woodwork, scrubbed floors and tidied up the mess left by the painters. Mr Barker, on loan from the master's father's London house, stocked the wine cellar and pantries, and old Tim put up fresh wallpaper. None of us knew if the mistress would keep us on, but the uncertainty gave our days a holiday air, which was why we dared assemble in the drawing room in the first place.

We never dreamed our master would drop in on us unannounced.

Mr Barker was playing the piano and I led the songs – back home I was famous for my clear soprano. 'The English Jenny Lind' the boys called me. And so I was quite lost in the light-hearted ditty 'Now Is the Month of Maying', when suddenly the smiling faces of my fellow servants froze in horror. Slowly I turned to see three tall gentlemen, resplendent in evening clothes, regarding the lot of us with amusement.

Mr Barker jumped to his feet and bowed stiffly. 'Mr Shaw, I'm terribly sorry. We weren't expecting you this evening, sir.'

I'd not yet met my employer. He'd been as invisible to me as I was supposed to be to him. Yet when the most handsome of the three said, 'Don't trouble yourself, Barker, I'm glad to see you all enjoying yourselves,' and fixed his eyes directly on my person, my whole body tingled.

Mr Barker was the only miscreant to keep his wits. 'We'll be getting back downstairs, sir. May I bring refreshment?'

The master was still gazing at me. 'I suppose we could

do with another bottle of port. And I'd like this night-ingale to stay and sing us a few songs.'

Mr Barker, Alice and Tim vanished like phantoms, and I was left alone with the gentlemen, altogether too visible to their glittering eyes.

'Don't be frightened.' The master smiled. 'You have a lovely voice. You could be on the stage.'

I blushed. Back home some had suggested as much, but more as a taunt for 'putting on airs' when I sang.

The master seated himself at the piano and began to play a lively tune I didn't recognise.

'I didn't know you could play so well, Charles. Perhaps you should go on the stage yourself?' said the blond gentleman who sported a thin moustache, smirking.

'He only uses his talents to seduce married ladies, Sheldon,' said the tallest man, who had striking green eyes. 'I wonder if his own wife will prove equally irresistible?'

The master merely laughed.

As the gentlemen all seemed quite merry from drink, I inched toward the door, hoping to make my escape.

Alas, they hadn't forgotten me. Green Eyes caught me by the arm and pushed me playfully toward the piano. 'Don't run away from us, little bird.'

'Voice as sweet as a Lillie Langtry's,' the blond declared, his eyes sweeping over me as if I were some-thing good to eat.

The master was watching me too. With his sky-blue eyes and wheat-coloured hair, he was by far the most handsome.

'What's your name then?' he asked me gently.

'Irene, sir.'

'You're new in our family employ?'

'They took me on a few weeks ago to help get the house ready. But it's up to your missus if I stay,' I blurted out foolishly.

The blond gentleman slipped his arm around my waist. 'If you don't keep her, I will. How about a kiss from those heavenly lips, sweet bird?'

I turned my head away. I knew when a man was drunk, whether on French wine or public-house ale.

Fortunately the master came to my rescue. 'Your seduction might fare better with a bit more subtlety and a lot more respect, my good man. Now let the poor girl go.'

'If the lass were married, you'd sing a different tune, eh, Charles?'

The master glared at his friend and escorted me into the hall. 'I apologise. Usually they're good fellows, but they're acting rotten tonight. Perhaps you'll sing for me under more favourable circumstances?'

'Yes, sir.' Imprudent as it would surely be, the bold part of me very much wanted to.

'Goodnight, then, little nightingale.' With a smile, he

bowed over my hand and gave it a kiss as if I were a fine lady.

Long after I returned to my narrow bedroom in the attic, my flesh still tingled from his touch.

* * *

Not one week later, Mr Barker approached me while I was unpacking dishes in the servants' hall.

'The master is here, Irene, and he'd like you to join him in the drawing room.' I must have looked dismayed, for he added, 'I know Mr Charles's character well. He enjoys life as gentlemen do, but he's never disgraced a servant. His tastes run to married ladies of his own station.'

'So I've heard. I'm safe then?'

'Quite.'

The master's demeanour was very different from the night we met. He looked weary, but managed a smile when I joined him at the piano.

'What would you like to sing tonight, Irene?'

'Do you know "A Bird in a Gilded Cage", sir?'

He frowned. 'Unfortunately it reminds me too much of my own impending life sentence in a cage. How about another?'

'"She Was Poor But She Was Honest"?'

He looked at me curiously, then grinned. 'Oh, I see, you're pulling my leg, you clever girl. Well, I've no intention of ruining a poor, virtuous maid. I am a gentleman above all, by aspiration, if not by birth.'

I had to smile, although I was sure he was toying with me as well. 'How about a duet? "Tell Me, Pretty Maiden".'

Pleased with my suggestion, he immediately launched into the popular tune. '*Tell me, pretty maiden, are there any more at home like you?*'

To my surprise, the master had a bewitching tenor voice, pure and slightly sad. Looking back, I see this was the moment I gave him my heart.

'*There are a few, kind sir, but simple girls, and proper too,*' I sang back, striking a coy pose as I did back home with my friends. Together we sang the famous song of courtship and flirtatious jealousy, warming to our roles as if we were indeed top of the playbill on a music-hall stage.

When the song was done, the master beamed. 'That was jolly fun. We do harmonise well, don't we?' His blue eyes took on a mischievous glint. 'You know, I've just come up with a wonderful plan. For revenge.'

'Revenge against whom, sir?'

'Those two ill-mannered brutes you met the other night. I'm giving a small party at a restaurant next week to celebrate my last days of freedom before I'm married off for the glory of our merchant dynasty. You could sing for us. I'd rent you a pretty costume and they'd have no recourse but to fall to their knees in admiration and apology. It would serve them right.'

6

'It would, sir.' I tried not to seem too eager, but thus far life in the city had meant homesickness and doubt about the future. Suddenly it promised untold adventures at this very moment.

'We'd have to practise together every night.'

'I'm at your service, sir. Singing with you cheers me as well.'

He paused and studied my face. 'You're so lovely. You must have a young man waiting at home for you.'

The beguiling heat of his attention loosened my lips more than was perhaps wise. 'I do have an understanding with someone. He's a baker's apprentice, so we're not free to marry for a while.'

'Handsome, strapping lad, I'd wager?'

I nodded. That described my Paul well enough.

'He's a lucky man. I'll think of him if ever I'm tempted.' The master's fingers brushed my hand ever so lightly. 'Rest assured you'll return to him as untouched as the day you left.'

The words themselves were soothing but his voice, dark and slow as molasses, hinted at unspeakable sins of the flesh. I felt a shudder – a sweet shudder – deep in my private places. I knew then I was no longer safe with him. Worse still, I was glad.

My adventure in the city had begun.

* * *

7

I wonder now if the master had planned it from the start, the path of degradation that gave me more pleasure than I'd ever known in my eighteen years? Not that he ever forced himself upon me. It was my own lust that drove me, one willing step at a time.

The following evening, when he requested one chaste kiss by the piano, I was the one to open my lips to him. I was the one who trembled with gladness when his mouth moved to my neck and uttered no protest when he fondled my bosom with his large, warm hands. He was the one to pull back panting and dishevelled, to send me off to a lonely bed out of respect to my betrothed.

The next afternoon we went to a theatrical shop in Covent Garden, where he had me fitted in a blue satin 'songbird' dress for the party. It was I who suggested a private showing of the new frock upon our return to the house. The costume was too low over the bosom and too high above the ankle to be respectable, but in the privacy of his dressing room the effect was most dramatic. The master showered me with the compliments that good manners had forbidden in the shop – how the dress exposed to advantage my divine décolletage and alabaster legs. Intoxicated by the homage, I pulled off the dress and bared my breasts fully to him. He stammered and swore he'd never seen a vision more lovely, snow kissed with berries. Then he suckled them while we lay on the daybed, until I begged him to take me. Once again, he withdrew, invoking my baker's apprentice.

To be honest, I'd nearly forgotten Paul. He existed in an innocent past I might possibly return to one day, where aunts warned against honey-tongued seducers and honest girls found transcendence only in prayer. Now my greatest desire was to make the master lose *his* honour and become mine for a precious moment before marriage took him from me for ever.

Finally, he gave me a reward for my devotion. I was wrapped in his arms on the daybed, drunk on his kisses, when he shyly asked me to confess what liberties I'd allowed my sweetheart to take with my fair body.

I immediately stiffened. I'd never spoken such things aloud before.

'Don't be shy, Irene, dear. I won't tell a soul.'

'Well, I let him kiss me, of course.'

'I suspected as much. Where did he kiss you?'

'My lips and … my bosom.'

'Nowhere else?'

'No.' Where else would there be?

He seemed rather disappointed at my purity. 'I know there's more, Irene. You're far too comfortable in a man's arms.'

I squirmed, oddly ashamed. 'We did lie together in bed when his parents were away. But I didn't let him undress me. He just held me and, well, he moved against me.'

9

The master's breath quickened. 'Did you touch his manhood with your sweet little hand?'

I began to realise it would be to my benefit to pretend I had. 'Well, yes, but please don't tell anyone. I'd die of shame.'

'My lips are sealed, my dear. Did you like touching it?'

'Yes. It was, um, very long.' It seemed the proper thing to say.

The master sighed and pressed himself closer. 'Tell me, Irene, did he spend? In your hand, perhaps, or elsewhere on your person?'

'Why must we speak of him, sir?' It was not so much the lewd questions but the silvery gleam in the master's eye that discomfited, even as it aroused me.

He kissed my forehead. 'Don't you know? If a woman has already done something with one lover, it's no longer a sin with the next.'

I'd heard a thousand rules about how a girl should comport herself with a man, but never this one. Suddenly my handsome master's preference for married ladies began to make sense. Perhaps I could turn this queer lovers' game to my advantage?

'I'm ashamed to say where he did it, sir,' I whispered into his shoulder.

'You can tell me. I know all about what healthy young men and women do together. And I'm sure your beau has very healthy appetites.'

'Will you say it for me then, sir?'

I felt his manhood twitch against my thigh. 'Very well. Did he spend in your beautiful mouth?'

It was all I could do not to gasp. I'd never dreamed of such an act, and yet immediately my cheeks tingled with a perverse desire to be filled with the hard baton imprisoned in my beloved's trousers.

'Yes, in my mouth,' I lied, 'but it was only once. I felt so ashamed and clumsy.'

'There, there, we all improve with practice.'

I took a deep breath. 'May I practise with you, sir?'

He laughed softly. 'You have become shameless, haven't you? Still, the French way is a useful method to please a man when you don't want a child. Your beau was honourable to suggest it, so I in turn would be honoured to help you refine your skills for him.'

Thus I found myself kneeling between the master's naked thighs, in a most intimate congress with his male member. Half of me wanted to close my eyes in terror, the other half wanted to study it like a schoolbook: the ruddy, rigid pole rearing up from the cushion of hair, the purplish head that poked through the folds at the top. My belly was in a knot, excitement mixed with fear. Could he tell I'd told a fib?

His unfailing gentlemanly courtesy soon calmed me.

'Kiss it first. Gently. That's right. Now take it in your mouth. Just the tip.'

My lips stretched around his knob. Down between my legs, my other mouth contracted in sympathy.

'That's good. Now slowly, up and down. You remember well. Is this how he liked it?' Gazing down at me with lust-veiled eyes, he rocked his hips up, pushing his cock deeper into my willing orifice. 'You may feel like choking, but just relax your throat. Good girl. Very good.'

Never had I done anything so bestial, so decadent. Never had anything brought such dark pleasure. My master was finally in *my* power.

'Put your hand around the bottom and hold it fast. Now move up and down, hand and lips together. Oh, God, yes.'

He arched back, his eyes squeezed shut.

'Harder, suck it harder.'

My jaw was sore, but I persevered, revelling in the way the fleshy tube responded to my attentions.

'Harder, oh, Jesus Christ Almighty.'

The shaft jerked between my lips. Hot, bitter liquid filled my mouth, and I fought the impulse to spit, forcing myself instead to swallow it down like a good girl takes medicine. The master groaned and pawed my hair, then went slack like a puppet.

I furtively wiped the last drops of male essence from my chin.

'Come here, you darling girl.' He hugged me close as if he'd never release me. 'Lips like heaven, that's what

12

you have. Only your second time and you're better than the whores in Paris.'

By and by, he asked if my betrothed had shown me the French way to please a woman.

'He started to, but his mother came back from the market too soon.' What else could I say? I was desperate to know that mysterious art.

'Then I'll carry on where he left off,' he said, peeling away my drawers and putting his own heavenly lips to my secret female place. His tongue darted between my nether lips, probing the softness until I let out a cry of delight. Next he began to lick me there as you might a strawberry ice at a country fair, up and down, up and down, with unflagging ardour. A pressure was building in my belly, like a fire, crackling and wild. The fire blazed higher, then suddenly shattered in my womb into a thousand tiny flames. I writhed like a madwoman as an invisible fist closed and opened between my legs.

When I came back to my senses, the master was smiling down at me.

'You're a natural, you know. I wonder if you'd be my accomplice in another naughty scheme to put my friends in their proper place. Would you like to hear it?'

Still floating in carnal bliss, I nodded. After all, I could always refuse.

* * *

The room at the restaurant was undoubtedly furnished for after-dinner *amour* with its spacious daybed, a wingback chair and a washbowl for intimate ablutions. There I put the finishing touches to my second costume: a pretty nightgown and velvet wrapper, with my hair brushed down over my shoulders like a fine lady about to retire to her bed.

But my duties for the evening had only begun. I realised I was trembling. I'd sung well enough, but I was still a novice at this kind of performance. I gave myself courage by remembering that this was my wedding gift to Charles, an offering he'd treasure more than the finest silver or French porcelain.

There was a knock at the door.

I hurried to open it.

Standing before me was my master's blond friend, Mr Sheldon Maxwell.

'Oh, my, I *am* the lucky winner,' he drawled, raising his eyebrows at my suggestive attire.

'Come in, sir,' I said, smiling bashfully. 'Please take a seat.'

'Did I win a private concert?' He settled into the leather chair, his male excitement already evident to my discerning eye.

'More than that, sir. You've won a trip to France.' I knelt before him and smiled into his eyes. He looked confused, which made me brave. 'May I take down your trousers?'

'What's this then?'

'You said you wanted me to kiss you, sir.'

'That I did.' Chuckling, he lounged back in the chair and let me attend to him, the confusion now turned most thoroughly to lust.

First I fondled his long, slim cock and bollocks, until he stood stiffly at attention. Then I kissed his mighty soldier, starting at the base and moving slowly toward the sensitive helmet. Mr Maxwell seemed to enjoy this very much, for he whimpered and grabbed the arms of the chair. Finally I took the knob in my mouth, swirling my tongue around it.

'Good God, girl, he's trained you well,' he hissed.

In reply, I slid my lips all the way down, sucking gently. Since I'd practised with the master over a dozen times in the past few days, my skills were far more assured.

Mr Maxwell groaned and shifted in the chair.

After that it didn't take long. I bobbed over him just a few times before he spent helplessly down my throat.

Well schooled as I was in the art, I didn't spill a drop.

My blood racing with my first taste of victory, I tidied myself up and waited for the next knock.

I knew it would be Green Eyes, known to society as Mr. John Davis. This gentleman seemed more at ease in my presence. He smirked at my nightdress and fingered the pile of towels on the washstand with an appreciative grunt.

'Stingy old Charles said I couldn't have you below the waist, but everything above is mine to enjoy as I desire. There was also something about a trip to France?'

'Paris, sir.' I gave him a saucy look. If the master had primed this one for the game, so would I play it. 'The boat departs when you take down your trousers.'

'Indeed, but first I'd like you to take off that wrapper and open your nightgown for me. Only to the waist of course.'

I blushed, but willed myself to untie the ribbons down the front of the nightgown with a steady hand.

Green Eyes took the liberty of pulling the nightgown down over my shoulders to expose my bosom to his satisfaction.

'Now let's go to Paris, little Irene.'

This gentleman's manhood was shorter, but quite robust. While I pleasured him, he called out a series of commands – 'slow now', 'use your tongue all around', 'take it deeper'–all the while kneading my bosom and flicking my nipples to points with his thumbs. Finally he barked, 'Stop there, girl.'

Timidly I obeyed. Had he not enjoyed my ministrations?

On the contrary, as if possessed, the gentleman quickly pushed me back on the floor and straddled my waist. He began to rub himself furiously, his rod poised over my chest. I watched in fascination as a pearl of liquid appeared at his tiny blind eye. In the next moment, he shouted out a rude word again and again as he sprayed his burning spunk all over my breasts.

In the end, Mr Davis did have the courtesy to mop me clean most gently with a towel from the washstand.

Thus was I flushed with two triumphs when the master walked through the door. He embraced me as if we'd been apart for years. Laughing with delight, I pulled him to the bed and we lay entwined together while I told him everything that had passed. He caught his breath when I revealed how Mr Maxwell kissed my mouth deeply afterwards, as if to savour the taste of his own mettle. And my darling groaned and held me tight when I described the way Mr Davis made a naughty mess all over my bubbies.

'You see, my love, I've had the soup and roast, but I'm still hungry for my pudding. It's your turn to submit to these lips that were the undoing of your old friends. Oh, how those brazen gentlemen sang for me in the end – swearing and grunting and crying out as they spent. We turned the tables, sir, we did indeed.'

'Oh, God, yes, Irene, show me just how you pleased them.' The master was quivering like a jelly, but his manhood was as rigid as an iron bar. I took that dear appendage in my mouth and sucked it like the sweetest candy. Time and time again, I brought him to the brink of spending, then pulled him back again until he sobbed for mercy. At last, I relented and gave him the hard sucking he craved for his climax.

And I let my favourite relish linger in my mouth for some time before I swallowed.

'Lips like heaven,' he whispered afterwards. 'I swear no woman has ever understood me as you do, darling. But I must tell you ...'

'I know, Charles, our time will be over when you marry, but I'm still yours for three days more.'

He laughed. 'Oh, no, my little nightingale, I won't give you up now. Mine is no love match, and many a married man before me has made special accommodation for his true heart's desire. Indeed I've come up with a wonderful plan. Would you like to hear it?'

Basking in his gaze, which saw me and loved me for all that I was, I knew I could refuse him nothing.

The Engagement Party
Alegra Verde

His hand was heavy, hard, and easily spanned the width of my backside. I closed my eyes against the quick, stinging slaps. The heat that suffused my face matched the throbbing burn that was spreading across my bare bottom. I was mortified. My curiosity, as usual, had got the best of me and I'd allowed this thing to go too far. I moved to rise, my hands gripping his hard wool-clad thigh, but the large hand that had been resting on my back, the feel of its weight enough to keep me still, pressed down firmly just as another stinging slap sliced at my bottom. The sound seemed to reverberate. I tensed. The long-fingered hand fell again, three times in rapid succession. To keep from crying out, my fingers gripped and twisted the thick stitching at the rim of the settee's cushion, and the fabric of his trousers. I could feel the white-hot stripes it left. The walls of my sex began to

19

clench, and the flesh began to swell and grow moist. I squirmed restlessly and the hand at my back grew heavier.

Embarrassed by the growing dampness between my legs, I buried my face in the thick, dark cloth, only vaguely aware that it was the tail of his evening jacket. My teeth scraped my lower lip and held on. Tears crowded my eyes and I couldn't breathe. The flat of his hot hand fell again, and his fingers slipped between the high round cheeks of my bottom, their tips sliding down to tease my slick opening, a brief reprieve before the sting came again. A tear slipped through a lash and ran the length of my cheek. The scalding hand fell again and the tips of my breasts tightened as the red heat streaked through my body. My heart beat faster and the soaking folds of my sex throbbed.

In the other room, a low reedy flute was playing Waltz No. 1 from Mozart's *Three Waltzes*, the cello close behind, trying to catch up; both seemed lost in time and tempo. The harsh pulse of hot hand against supple flesh was a far more thrilling music. I imagined the maze of long white marks his fingers had made on the reddened skin. A woman laughed, high and shrill. The brush of full skirts against narrow walls; the pungent smell of tobacco. The voices in the hall grew more distinct.

'Ward made short work of him, he did ...' The sound of a hoarse male voice made husky by years of smoke. A quiet laugh then the soft thump and swish of silk like a woman being pressed against wallpaper. The sounds drifted through the closed door, but the searing hand paid them no heed. Slap, piercing sting; I gasped, my fingers knotting then flexing against the coarse cloth. Slap, slap, and then a long slow throb. Two fingers pinched and twisted a bit of plump flesh high on my arse. The shock ran the length of my body, leaving me trembling. My sex pulsed and tightened. I could feel the moisture seeping. His hot palm and hard fingers burned against the flesh of my thighs; again, quick and sharp.

The image of the wooden rod my tutor used to use flashed on the inside of my closed lids. 'If you're going to be brazen enough to demand that you be allowed to study Latin, you should at least put forth an effort,' the bespectacled young man had barked as he wielded the thin length of wood. There was always the swishing sound and then the biting sting across my thighs. My breasts felt heavy and my nipples felt as though they were piercing the fabric of my bodice. I pressed my lips together, trying to suppress the moans. My fingers snagged between a layer of soft wool and coarser upholstery as I tried to bury my face, but sounds still escaped.

'It would have been a better fight in 1829. Byrne was in better shape two years ago.' The voice in the hall was light, playful and very female.

'What bloodlust! An hour and a quarter of raw knuckles and bruised ribs not enough for you?' the man's whiskey-smoked voice again.

'Shh, remember, I was never there.' Silence, the rustle of fabric pressed and sliding against the wallpaper, a moan. Long fingers slid down the crevice of my bottom and slipped in, through the wetness that seeped from my sex.

A giggle from the other room. 'Not here.' The shuffle of dancing shoes, the light click of heels on the wooden floor before the narrow strip of carpet claimed their sound. I trembled, my stomach pressing into the slightly open V of his lap.

'You like that, don't you?' he whispered, his voice cold like the sting that followed as he raised his hand and let it fall hard and tart against the fleshy rise of my arse. Again, and once more, harder, before he shoved me off his lap and I tumbled in a whirl of lace and taffeta to the carpet at his feet.

'You're Ethel's cousin Jen, are you not?'

I nodded.

'An unmarried girl of barely twenty.' His eyebrows were arched and high as he spoke. 'Are you accustomed to spending time alone with men who are not related?'

I shook my head while surreptitiously rubbing cool fingers over a particularly searing spot on my bottom, but I couldn't think. I was only aware of my stinging backside, the knowing tingle between my legs and the hard press of my nipples against the crisp corded pleats that ran the length of my bodice.

He stood over me. Tall. Long legs in slim trousers.

The brocade of his burgundy waistcoat beckoned me. I wanted to touch the thick swirling thread that made up its intricate design. I wanted to run my finger around the tight swirls and trail it down past the last gold button. It had worked its way free of its hole and shone like a brilliant jewel, a garnish at the bottom of his waistcoat that drew the eye to the two pointed tips of lush brocade. They framed and nearly touched the beginning of the long bulge that lay invitingly just beneath his waist, a plump sausage that trailed down to just inside his thigh. I reached out to touch it.

'No!' His voice was soft but firm, his eyes dark.

Someone laughed, a man, deep, throaty, followed by a peal of feminine giggles. The sounds wandered off down the hall.

I withdrew my hand.

He unbuttoned the placket, reached in and tugged until the tip and just a little more of his thickly swollen sex peeked out.

'Do you want to touch it?'

I nodded, unable to speak as the muscles of my sex trembled and my nipples hardened further, straining against the uneven fabric.

'Only your mouth,' he said and held the plum out to me.

Kneeling before him now, I leaned in and licked the purplish helmet. It was slightly salty and very warm.

There was a faint savoury smell, musky, like the sea in summer. His hand trembled, but he said nothing. I slipped my mouth over the hot little hood and sucked. I liked the way it felt in my mouth, all warm, round and slick. I sucked harder, making sure that my teeth only skirted the tender skin. He held more out to me and soon I had a good portion of him in my mouth. I gripped one of his thighs with one hand and the edge of a tight round cheek with the other while I sucked at him. I tasted as much of him as I could. My mouth slid up and down the heated skin; my tongue lingering over the notch under the hood and the places where the engorged veins made the skin rise and swell tightly.

He groaned and one of his hands fell to my head, his fingers sifting deeply through the tresses until they were snugly tucked into my curls, holding me in place but giving me enough room to continue sucking the ever-hardening length of him. The tugging way his fingers threaded through my hair reminded me of last summer, of the way Henry had held my head as we knelt near the pond.

Henry and I had grown up together as his father's estate abutted ours. We had spent the day together saying our goodbyes as he was leaving the following day for the requisite Grand Tour. He and I had always played like boys together, rough and tumble, and he didn't let up when I began wearing long skirts, although the play had become somewhat amorous on his part.

That afternoon, after some tumbling and much laughter, we had ended up sprawled on the grassy bank. I was flat on my back and his head was lost somewhere under my skirts. I whacked him with my fist to dislodge him, but I'm sure that the many layers of cloth stunted the blow because he continued to forage. His head nudged its way beneath my chemise and his teeth began to graze the sensitive skin of my inner thigh. An odd jolt ran the length of my body. I was so stunned and curious that I stilled, waiting for what might come next.

He continued on his way, licking and nibbling, until he reached my sex, which he began to lave with his tongue. It was an odd sensation, wet and raspy, not unlike the kiss of a big dog. I laughed and whacked him again, but he held my hips and continued. I didn't like the way his fingers dug into my hips or the afflicted way he was breathing. It sounded as though an ancient asthmatic was tangled beneath my skirts. I shoved him with all my might, kicked out at him and rolled away, leaving him panting a few yards off.

To add to my discomfiture, he had unbuttoned his pants and his manly part protruded from the opening, thin but long and obviously aroused.

'I need you,' he panted. 'I'll come back for you, I promise. Just let me put it into you for a moment,' he begged holding *it* in his right hand.

'I've no desire to marry you, Henry Ledbetter,' I said

with a laugh. He was a fool and obviously thought I was one of his pack.

'Well, you might at least lick it,' he grimaced. 'As I did you.'

I rolled my eyes at him and began to stand.

'Please,' he begged. Henry was like that, always coaxing me to try something new, and while it might have resulted in a twisted ankle or having to hide under a heap of soiled hay, it was always interesting. So I'd crawled over to him and examined the offering. It looked relatively clean, rather pink really. I'd leaned in to smell it and in his eagerness he jabbed the knobby point at me, grazing a nostril. It was damp and smelled of heat, boy and, oddly enough, grass. It was not unpleasant so I licked it and found its saltiness appealing. I let the knob slip between my lips and Henry groaned. I liked the smooth round head so I sucked it as I would a lemon drop, savouring its shape and tartness. That is when his hand gripped my head and held me there while he thrust once, twice, and then he cried out as he erupted inside my mouth. Stunned, I had fallen back on my bum, as had he.

But this was different. Although his fingers were threaded through my hair, he didn't hold me stiffly as Henry had. He let me move, suck and taste him freely, only increasing the pressure when he especially liked the way my tongue or lips felt. Only then did he thrust into my mouth, and then it felt right, then I could suck him in earnest. I liked the way its smooth skin rode the roof of my mouth and the way he trembled against my lips. I liked the sounds that he made, husky moans of appreciation.

'You've done this before?' His voice was deep, throaty, almost hoarse.

I nodded and then shook my head, but did not relinquish the firm morsel between my lips. It hadn't been like this with Henry so I wasn't sure whether it counted. I wondered: if I sucked him hard enough, would he erupt as Henry had? Would it taste the same, hot, creamy and somewhat sticky?

His laugh was short and a bit strangled.

'Have you ever had a man's cock between your legs?' he asked, as his fingers slipped through my hair to my scalp, cupping my head as though to hold me more firmly.

That stopped me, the tip of the plum poised just between my lips. It was time to pull back, time to smooth my skirts down and scurry away. Had I been born male, I'd have had all manner of amorous adventures by now, but having been born female I knew and respected my limitations. Well, the most important ones. Although I had admittedly pressed the bar, I knew when to release it. As it stood, I didn't really know this man or his limits and he didn't know me. Based on my behaviour thus far, he had every right to believe that I was both experienced and loose – when in fact I'd vowed to save the finale for my marriage bed. Just how far would he press his advances? I couldn't very well risk crying out and being caught *in flagrante delicto*. So I sucked at the rounded tip once more, my tongue tracing the moist dimple at its centre before relinquishing it. I could still feel its shape in my mouth as I pressed my forehead into the warm wool of his hard thigh. His hand still in my curls was gentle for a moment and then it fisted around a clump of hair.

'A tease,' he said, tugging me up by my head and hair, his palm gradually opening to firmly cup my scalp, directing me until I was on my feet and standing before him. 'I should show you just what ...' His words were a harsh whisper, but he was buttoning his pants. When he was done, he took me by the arm and yanked me towards a plushly upholstered armchair, where he summarily pushed me head first over its thickly padded arm. Briefly, I flailed about with my arms outstretched and my hands grabbing clumsily at the cushions, struggling to regain my balance, frightened but more than a little curious. Layers of cloth fell heavily over my head as he plucked my skirts from where they had moulded to my bottom and then tossed them out of the way. A brief waft of cool air assailed my bare nether cheeks just as the sting of his hot palm began its assault again. Stunned, my sex twitched, but I squirmed, trying to burrow through the layers of skirt, eager to find light. My bottom burned from the barrage of angry smacks.

'Un-mar-ried-girls-should-not-play-grown-up-games-with-men.' A pointed slap accompanied each syllable.

His fingers slid lower, slipping into the wetness that seemed to spill from between my legs and coat my sex. I could feel the heat suffusing my face. Discomfited, I struggled harder to free myself from my skirts, but a hand pressed, then neatly splayed against my waist to hold me in place. Another sting and then his fingers slowed, dipping low, sliding down along the swollen lips of my sex, lingering and exploring its slippery crevices. A finger and then a thumb found a particularly sensitive bit of flesh and began to strum it. Even as I tried to scoot away, he kept coming, finding and teasing the deep wet place until a series of waves like a sustained shiver began to rise from the place where his fingers tarried. I shivered as ... tremors and icy tingles rose, just there, and there, wherever he touched, moments of incoherence, tiny knots of delirium ... and then a tremulous pulse swooshed, rushing upwards and through my centre. I closed my eyes and tightened my thighs, almost involuntarily, around his fingers as I tried to brace myself. Unable to hold it at bay, I buried my face in the silk upholstery and gripped the chair's edge, my body twisted and tight as it crashed over and through me, leaving me tingling and without air to breathe.

Still trembling in its aftermath, I managed to struggle up, my head finally emerging from its blanket of skirts. Suddenly, I was tumbling sideways and landing in a sprawl of lace and pink taffeta at his feet again. He took a step away, dodging the delicate fabric as I ended on my backside, my fluff of a dress modestly covering all but a long line of sheer silk-covered legs and daisy-sprigged garters. A smile crossed his lips as he glimpsed the garters; the tips of his fingers met his nose and he inhaled deeply. The familiar bulge at his thigh seemed to lengthen. Just as suddenly, the smile faded and he glared down at me.

He watched me for another moment, and then he took a step backwards, pursed his lips and turned towards the door.

'Let that be a lesson to you,' he huffed. He did not look back as he stepped out into the corridor and pulled the door closed.

* * *

How had I come to be in such a predicament? I told myself that I had come merely to apologise for causing the last bottle of his favourite port to shatter. He'd been so crestfallen when it had crashed to the floor, and he'd been so terribly handsome when his full lips had made that astonished O, a dark lock of hair falling forwards as he glared down at the pool of ruby liquid. He'd looked up from the pieces of broken glass and frowned at me, a scowl that said I had deprived him of his final joy, but he quickly recovered his manners and turned away.

'That was the last bottle! It cost more than a month of your wages,' he had shouted rudely at the poor servant, who had immediately fallen to his knees and with a hastily retrieved napkin had begun to dab at the spreading stain on the carpet. 'I shall take it out of your wages. Better yet, you are dismissed. I'm sure we can find someone who can get a bottle of wine from the cellar to the table without incident.' The red-faced servant was still on his knees dabbing and carefully placing shards of green glass on a silver tray when his master had stormed out of the room.

I hadn't wanted him to punish the servant, as the incident had been my fault. Seeking refuge from one of my more ardent suitors, I had stumbled upon the bridegroom as he sought a moment of privacy in a comfortable corner of the library. He was quite striking standing there before the fire, his arm resting on the mantel, his head lowered as though he sought a moment to revive his wits after the rigours of introductions to his prospective in-laws, of dancing with matrons and charming the family patriarch. I had witnessed his charm, his easy laughter, and how it drew others to him. In my haste to flee my wayward thoughts of the brooding gentleman, I had blindly collided with the tray-bearing footman. In order to avoid trampling me, the servant had sacrificed the port.

After assuring the shaken footman that I would placate his master, I'd gone in search of the angry bridegroom. I found the sombre gentleman sipping what appeared to be a whiskey, neat, in the solitude of an unused sitting room.

'It was my fault, the wine,' I stammered. 'You mustn't punish the footman.'

He took his time assessing me and then he smiled and nodded. 'Would you care to take his licks?'

My damp hands grappled with the fabric of my skirts. I remembered the first time I'd seen him in Lady Latham's garden. He'd had the young widow over his lap, her skirts rucked up around her waist, her bright pink bum in the air as his hand rose high and landed hard. I'd come bearing lemon scones, a particular favorite of Grace Latham's. I wouldn't say that she and I are friends, but we are neighbours and her conversation can be diverting. She and the bride are contemporaries and it was at one of Grace's gatherings that the bride and groom were introduced. As I made my way through the back gardens, I had heard moaning, but nothing prepared me for the sight of the long-legged young man with his hand on Lady Latham's naked bottom. Stunned, I tripped and fell on my backside, scattering scones. However, instead of fleeing, I had hidden, ducking behind the shrubbery to watch.

'If it would save him from further punishment,' I offered, wondering if he was teasing or being ironic. Then he sat up straighter, one palm splayed on the seat cushion of the armless settee, the other still holding his drink as he perused the length of me again before beckoning me towards him with a crooked finger. Taking one of my hands in his, he held it lightly as he placed his glass on the floor beneath the seat. Well, I had agreed to the punishment; what could I do? Before I could think twice, he had pulled me belly first across his lap and tossed up my skirts. After a cursory brush of warm fingers against warmer skin, he was spanking my bare bottom.

I was all at once appalled, frightened and, yes, titillated. Images flashed before me of Lady Latham's rosy bottom, of her squirming on his lap, of the intense look on his face, of the way his tongue darted out to wet his lips as his hand fell. I wanted to see and feel what he would do next. Would he touch me as he touched her? How far would he take it? How far would I let him? I liked the feel of his huge hand as it splayed across my bottom. I liked the sting and release, the way it made the lips down there twitch. I wondered if he really punished his servants in this way – maybe the females. I wondered if they did things, spilled the gravy on his shirt or failed to keep the fireplace in his rooms lit, so he would call them to task. I couldn't imagine him doing this to the footman. But I could imagine my hand on his bottom, firm and round.

33

I might slap it lightly unless he begged me to make it harder. My hand would sting and grow warm, and the sounds of his groans would make me wet. When he'd finally mounted Lady Latham, I had watched the way his backside rose and fell, the way his sac swayed as it hung heavy between his thighs. I wanted to touch him then, to slide my hand over his smooth arse, to cup his sac, but I just held my breath and watched.

Maybe he'd chosen this method of punishment to humiliate me. Although my heart raced and, admittedly, I was a little frightened, I didn't feel humiliated. I opened my legs slightly, just so, and hoped that he would touch me there, where I felt all wet and wanting. Even though I was certain that this was not the proper way to behave with one's almost married host, I wanted to feel the slide of his fingers just so, just there, and he seemed willing to oblige. However, now he seemed truly angry, having left me crumpled on the floor without even offering me a hand up.

My bottom was still tingling and the flesh between my legs was aquiver as I clutched at an armchair for support, then stood and went about righting my clothing. He was an odd one, and I couldn't help but smile, as I had enjoyed our little sport. I had no doubt that our brief tryst would remain a secret between the two of us, as the soon-to-be-wed groom would be as reticent as I. I, of course, wished him and my cousin Ethel the best. She'd been on the shelf for several years and had finally given in and decided to buy herself a husband, a very delectable one at that, tall, dark and with very large and powerful ... hands, and a strong will. I had to commend his restraint, as I was quite tempted to throw caution to the wind and my legs in the air. Although I knew Ethel was never one to share, I hoped that there would be another opportunity to bare my bottom before her alluring fiancé. Meanwhile, I checked my face in the glass of a nearby watercolour, a still life of fresh fruit with bowl, fluffed my skirts and headed back into the fray of the engagement party.

Hitting the Right Notes
Rose de Fer

Lily positions her fingers on the keys, gently, as though she is afraid of damaging them. She hesitates another second, then takes a deep breath and presses down. The piano responds, not with music but with a frightful racket. I wince, biting my lip.

She quickly corrects her error but Mr Blackshaw is frowning.

'I'm sorry, sir,' she says softly, lowering her head. Her hands flutter to her lap like frightened animals and she presses them into her pinafore, every inch the demure little chambermaid.

Mr Blackshaw is quiet for a moment. Then he simply says, 'Again.'

Lily straightens her back and lifts her hands, arranging them on the keys once more, stretching her fingers to reach what must be a difficult chord. This time it sounds more like music when she attacks the keys and I can tell she feels a little more confident. She finds her way into the piece and I listen as she plays. It's soft and sweet, just like her. I'm no expert but to me it sounds heavenly.

Mr Blackshaw, however, is unimpressed. He raps Lily smartly across the knuckles with his ruler. I gasp in concert with her and cover my mouth lest my own noise attract his displeasure. Fortunately, it all seems reserved for his pupil, who cowers beside him like a flower withering in a storm. Wisps of hair have come loose from her lacy mob cap and she smoothes them away from her face before making another attempt at the piece. But it's no use. She's lost the trick of it.

'Appalling,' Mr Blackshaw says. The room seems full of the stony silence that follows. Lily looks almost relieved when he tells her sharply to begin again.

By this time her hands are trembling so much she can barely place her fingers on the right keys. She takes a deep shuddering breath but before she can start to play Mr Blackshaw finds fault with her posture.

'And don't slouch. Do you think Chopin imagined this piece played in such a fashion? By young ladies who can't even be bothered to sit up straight and who clearly have no respect for his music?'

Lily has no answer for that. She lowers her head submissively as he chastises her.

'I'm trying to make something of you, young lady. Or don't you want to be more than just a chambermaid?'

'I do, sir, it's just –'

'I like to instil a sense of culture in my servants, to smooth out the rough edges. But it seems like I'm wasting my time with you.'

Lily whimpers as though struck. 'But sir,' she protests, 'I have practised, honest! It's just … it's a difficult piece.'

'Of course it's difficult. I'm hardly going to set you something easy to learn, am I? Or perhaps you'd prefer that? Some simple little nursery rhyme? Something you can peck out with two fingers like an infant?'

'But I can't –'

'Stand up.'

'Sir?'

'You heard me, Lily. Stand up.'

I hear her swallow as she slowly rises to her feet, head well down, her face flushed with shame. My own face burns in sympathy but I wouldn't take her place. I stand still, as I have been instructed, a silent witness to her disgrace. But her nervousness is infectious and my fingers pluck at the velvet ribbons of my gown. The brocade skirt rustles softly, earning me a warning glance from Mr Blackshaw. I stop at once and fold my hands in front of me, the perfect lady.

Mr Blackshaw turns back to Lily. He taps the cushioned piano bench with his ruler and she gives him one final beseeching look before obeying the unspoken command. I press my legs together as she assumes the familiar position, gently placing first one knee and then the other on the piano bench. She kneels there like a penitent, her hands resting lightly on the keys as Mr Blackshaw raises her black uniform skirt and tucks it into the strings of her pinafore.

Her undergarments barely conceal her as it is but Mr Blackshaw wants her fully exposed, humiliated. He unties the drawstring that fastens her pantalettes around her waist. They fall open like the petals of a flower, revealing her soft round bottom and the pink lips of her sex.

The position forces her back into a graceful arch although I can see the strain in her thighs as she keeps her bottom raised up. She is not allowed to sit on her heels. Mr Blackshaw makes that clear with one warning tap from the ruler.

'Now,' he says coolly, 'we'll see if you can't perform a little better now. You may begin when you're ready.'

I hold my breath while I wait for her to find the courage for another attempt. I know she'll fail. Sure enough, she hits a wrong note in the very first chord. Bravely she tries to play through it but there's no recovering from such a disastrous mistake. Eventually the notes trail away and she bows her head in disgrace.

This time Mr Blackshaw doesn't say a word. He steps purposefully to one side and lays the ruler against the smooth pale flesh of her bottom. A little shudder runs through Lily's body and she holds perfectly still for him as he raises the ruler and brings it down with a sharp crack across both cheeks.

I edge a little to the side so I may see her face as well. Her eyes are closed and she bites her lip to keep from crying out. Mr Blackshaw doesn't like her to make a fuss.

The second stroke elicits a whimper and she tosses her head with a gasp. Her fingers twitch but she knows better than to bang the keys in response to the pain. She wriggles a little and I can see two vivid pink stripes rising across her flesh, flaring and deepening. They might be the brush strokes of a painter.

Lily tenses in anticipation of another stroke and Mr Blackshaw leaves her in suspense for several seconds before delivering it. This one is harder than the others. This one makes her yelp and she drums her legs on the cushion.

My breath catches in my throat at the sight, at the shock of bright pain she feels in such an intimate area. For I am no stranger to it myself. My bottom tingles at the memory of my own such punishments. The slice of the cane, the kiss of the rod, the smack of a hard hand. All of it makes me squirm. All of it makes me wet.

It has the same effect on Lily, whose pouting sex glistens with her own arousal as the ruler finds its mark again. I bite my lip, feeling lightheaded as I imagine myself comforting her, stroking her tender pink cheeks. Kissing her ...

But only afterwards.

Now I must watch as she struggles to maintain her position. Her cap has come away and her hair falls in soft waves around her pretty face. I love seeing her in disarray, all her dignity stripped away, her vulnerability laid bare. My sex throbs in response as she whimpers and yelps, flinching at each stroke. When at last the punishment is over I have to remind myself to breathe.

'Now then, Lily,' Mr Blackshaw says, his voice a little kinder now that she has been corrected, 'shall we try it again?'

'Yes, sir,' she whispers.

Her legs tremble with the effort of holding her position as she arranges her fingers on the keys once more. This time she doesn't hesitate. This time the music that comes forth is note-perfect. Beautiful. I close my eyes, listening, letting it flow over me. The lovely little song might be her cool hands caressing my naked skin, perhaps soothing away the pain of my own chastisement for some trivial misdemeanour.

She brings the piece to an end and waits to hear his verdict.

He is smiling. 'Very good, Lily. Very good indeed.'

She smiles too, her face radiant with pride at having

satisfied her demanding taskmaster. 'Thank you, sir,' she murmurs.

He takes her arm and helps her up. After kneeling for so long her legs wobble and it takes her a moment to find her feet. Mr Blackshaw doesn't allow her to adjust her drawers or her skirt, however, and as she turns around I have a good view of the scarlet canvas of her bottom. The red is a startling contrast to the black of her skirt and the white of her pinafore and pantalettes. She looks over at me and I blush as she gives me a lascivious wink, all her shyness gone now.

I feel my nipples tighten beneath the heavy gown and I suddenly sense Mr Blackshaw's eyes on me. His gaze might be a hand beneath my skirt for the wave of desire that overwhelms me. My sex pounds with need. Mr Blackshaw turns to Lily, who returns his look with a mischievous grin. Then they both hold out a hand to me.

I step forward nervously, as though onto a stage, surrendering my hands to them. They lead me from the music room and up the main staircase. When we reach the bedroom Mr Blackshaw shuts the door and Lily goes at once to the mirror to admire her marks. She turns this way and that, wincing at the sight of her bright red bottom, touching it gingerly.

'Does it hurt terribly?' I ask.

Lily smiles. 'Oh, yes,' she says in a silky voice. 'Terribly.'

Heat floods my face as she takes my hand and presses it against the flaming red skin of her cheeks.

'And now it's your turn.'

I gasp. 'But ... But I ...' It's all I can think of to say. I can offer no reasonable defence.

Mr Blackshaw takes my arm and steers me towards the four-poster bed. The long skirt of my dress catches on the leg of a chair and for a moment I have the ludicrous fantasy that it might be enough to hold me back from their wicked intentions, that I might be trapped by the lavish garment and saved. But Lily tugs it free and gives me a firm push with a hand in the small of my back.

'You enjoyed watching that, didn't you?' Lily says, her voice husky in my ear.

I know better than to lie. My excitement is more than obvious. I am blushing all over, my breasts heaving within the confines of the tight bodice. I can hardly breathe.

'We can't have you swooning, my girl,' Mr Blackshaw says, placing a hand against my chest. My heart races beneath his palm. 'I think this dress had better come off.'

I squeeze my thighs together against the surge of lust this provokes but my fingers aren't up to the task. They fumble uselessly at the buttons before Lily tuts and pushes my hands away to do the job herself. And it is a job, undressing a lady.

First she removes the velvet jacket and lays it gently over the back of a chair. Then Mr Blackshaw begins to unfasten my skirt while Lily unhooks the myriad buttons of my high-collared white blouse. Next come the petticoats and bustle. Throughout the procedure I stand still and obedient, feeling more exposed with the removal of each piece of clothing.

Lily smiles up at me as she kneels to unlace my dainty little boots and then her fingers peel away the stockings. Now I'm wearing only a chemise, a corset and the same split-crotch pantalettes as Lily. While they cover each leg to the knee, they gape open in the back and I moan softly as the cool air teases my damp sex.

Mr Blackshaw bends down behind me and parts my cheeks with his fingers, peering closely at me.

I whimper, mortified.

'Goodness me,' he says with mock disapproval, 'this is hardly befitting of a lady, is it?'

I know there's no answer for that. My excitement is more than obvious. I daren't point out that I'm not the only one in such a state.

Without another word he gestures towards the ottoman at the foot of the bed. I beg him with my eyes but he is implacable. I kneel there and Lily positions my arms, raising them out to the sides so I can take hold of the bedposts. I'm grateful for the extra support as Mr Blackshaw bends me forwards, positioning me how he wants me. He unfastens my drawers as he did Lily's and they fall open to either side. They stay gathered around my knees, however, hobbling me. I like the thought that I couldn't run away even if I wanted to.

I close my eyes and hold my breath, bracing myself for the punishment that is sure to follow. Instead I feel Mr Blackshaw's hands at my waist and I sigh with gratitude as he begins to untie the laces of the corset.

Lily crawls onto the bed on all fours and watches, a catlike grin on her face. It's a slightly wicked grin and I realise their intention as soon as Mr Blackshaw gives the laces a firm tug. I clutch the bedposts so I am not yanked to the floor. Then I gasp as Mr Blackshaw draws the laces even tighter and my waist shrinks another inch.

'Nice,' Lily purrs, drawing a finger across the swell of my bosom above the corset. 'Very nice indeed.'

My face burns at the combined sense of constriction and exposure as the tight-laced corset makes even more of a display of my breasts and bottom. But, as if that isn't enough, Mr Blackshaw places the ruler between my bare thighs, smacking them gently to urge them apart. I catch a glimpse of myself in the mirror out of the corner of my eye. It's a positively lewd sight and I blush and lower my head, relishing the sense of shame and excitement.

'Now,' he says, 'what shall we do with you?'

He draws the edge of the ruler down over my naked bottom and I shiver at the touch of the cool wood.

'What does a naughty young lady deserve who gets so

shamefully wet at the sight of her maid being punished? Hmm?'

He can't possibly expect an answer to that. In any case, I'm incapable of speech. I make some tiny mewling sound and squirm, rolling my hips in an agony of desire and fear.

Lily moves closer to the edge of the bed and crouches right in front of me. 'I should think she deserves the same as her poor little maid,' she says, lifting my chin with a fingertip. 'Wouldn't you agree ... Miss?'

My face burns feverishly hot and I nod helplessly.

'Very well,' says Mr Blackshaw.

And before I can protest, before I can even prepare myself, he brings the ruler down smartly across my cheeks. I yelp, writhing and struggling as much as the position will allow me. Which isn't much. The corset won't let me bend at all; it thrusts my bottom out, making it even more of a target. And with my arms spread between the bedposts I might as well be chained like a slave for a whipping. I can't even kick my legs. Parted as they are, with my pantalettes down around my knees, I am fully restrained. Helpless. It's absolutely thrilling.

The ruler finds its mark again and I cry out, tossing my head and clutching the bedposts tightly. The stinging blows spread across my skin in stripes of pain and between my legs I feel myself getting even wetter. My sex tingles, desperate for attention.

Another stroke, then another. I gasp and yelp with each one but Mr Blackshaw is merciless. So is Lily. I lift my head to see her eyes glittering with devilish excitement. With a mischievous smile she strokes the swell of my bosom, teasing me as the ruler falls again.

Her fingers trail along the neck of my chemise, toying with the tiny laces. Deftly she unties them and peels open the flimsy garment. I whimper as she eases my breasts free of their confinement, exposing me fully. She kisses me then, her lips warm and wet against my nipples. The added stimulation makes me lightheaded and for a moment I am afraid I will faint. The ruler revives me.

Lily strokes and kisses my breasts, pleasuring me while Mr Blackshaw punishes me. The twin sensations mingle and blend like some rare and decadent concoction and I am lost somewhere in between. I feel Lily's teeth close gently around my nipple and I hiss with pain. Then Mr Blackshaw's hand is between my legs, stroking me softly.

'Oh, dear,' he says with a smile in his voice. 'I'm afraid that hasn't done any good at all. If anything she's even wetter.'

Lily grins at me. 'Shocking,' she says.

I can't help but smile myself at their outrageous hypocrisy. A glance over my shoulder shows me the bulge in Mr Blackshaw's trousers and we both know what state Lily is in.

'Take me.'

They are silent for a moment, exchanging a surprised look as if they had forgotten I had a voice. It isn't much of one but I use it again, whispering my demand.

'Take me. Please.'

Lily moves first, gathering my breasts in her soft hands and tweaking both nipples as she presses her lips to mine. I close my eyes and hear Mr Blackshaw unfastening his trousers. Then his hands are on my bottom and I gasp at the pain as he strokes my cruelly punished flesh. He draws his fingers over the angry red weals, making me pant as he teases me. At last he makes his way lower, slipping his fingers down to my soft wet sex.

Then I feel the warm hardness of his cock pressing against me. I tremble, my arms straining with the effort of maintaining my position, and he enters me. He slides his length inside me with one long slow thrust. I moan as the sensation spreads through my entire body, wave upon wave of pleasure. I push myself back against him, urging him deeper. He obliges, taking hold of my tiny pinched waist and thrusting hard. I wriggle my sore bottom against him, clenching myself around his cock. All the while Lily is lavishing her own attention upon me, pinching, kissing, licking. The onslaught of stimulation is nearly unbearable.

It isn't long before I feel myself about to climax. The sensation begins to build in my sex, growing more intense with each powerful thrust. And just when I think I can't take any more, my body explodes. Ecstasy washes over me, leaving me breathless. I go limp, shuddering with bliss, every nerve in my body wildly alive and pulsing and sending little shock waves of pleasure through me.

It takes me some time to recover, to realise that Mr Blackshaw is still fucking me, prolonging my own climax while he reaches his own. Lily is frigging herself under her skirt, her legs splayed obscenely in front of me as she watches us. I'm too devastated to do anything but bask in the delicious obscenity of it all and when Mr Blackshaw comes he clutches me tightly, emptying himself into me while Lily muffles her own cries, screaming into a pillow as her body bucks and arches on the bed.

My head is spinning. My body aches from the position but I don't want to move. I listen to the birds chirping outside, the wind rustling the leaves in the trees. I feel part of a strange and beautiful world. A horse whinnies and I smile as the clip-clop of hooves on cobblestones draws near. I imagine what it might be like to be harnessed like that, to be urged on with a riding crop, to have a tail –

'Oh, no!'

Lily's cry yanks me rudely from my fantasy. Her eyes are wide as she scrambles up off the bed and runs to the window. Outside I hear the carriage draw to a halt, the horses stamping their feet.

'My father!' Lily wails, her face ashen. 'Hurry! Mary, dress yourself!'

It takes me a moment to remember my place. My true place, that is. But as Lily – Miss Lily, I have to remind myself – strips off and thrusts my black dress and pinafore at me, the mist begins to clear.

Mr Blackshaw quickly does up his trousers and hauls me to my feet. I'm still a little dazed as I fumble with the buttons of my uniform and try to smooth my hair into some semblance of order. I spend a few moments looking around for my little lace cap but it is nowhere to be found.

Together Mr Blackshaw and I manage to get Lily back into her dress. Although it's obvious to us that she isn't wearing much underneath, her father is unlikely to spot the impropriety. Her hair is another story but perhaps she can cover it with a bonnet. There's no more time. The master is back and we exchange a horrified look as he calls for the butler.

'Blackshaw? I say, are you here?'

Mr Blackshaw hurries out, regaining his composure with every step. It takes me a little longer. I trail behind him, following him into the music room, where His Lordship stands looking perplexed.

'Ah, there you are, Blackshaw,' he says. If he thinks it odd that his butler wasn't there to open the front door he doesn't say anything. 'Such a funny thing happened. I got to Lord and Lady Carlson's estate only to find that they hadn't asked me to come at all. It's damned peculiar.'

'Indeed, sir,' says Mr Blackshaw, unflappable as always.

His Lordship shrugs it off. 'Anyway, how's my daughter getting on with her lessons?'

'Very well, sir. Perhaps she might play something for you this evening.'

'Oh, I don't much care, if I'm to be honest,' he says dismissively. 'But it's jolly good of you to take the time to help her. One hates to see a young lady with nothing to do. Idle hands and all. Next thing you know they're reading novels and getting all manner of unsuitable ideas.'

'Indeed.' Mr Blackshaw glances over at me and I have to avert my eyes lest the amusement in his make me laugh.

'What the devil?' His Lordship reaches down to pick something up from the floor by the piano. A scrap of lace.

I gasp. 'Oh! I'm sorry, sir, I must have lost it while Miss Lily was practising. Mr Blackshaw was kind enough to let me listen. She does play beautifully, sir. Like the very angels.'

His Lordship smiles at my inane prattle as he hands me back my cap. 'Ah. Well, jolly good.'

'Begging your pardon, sir, but I'll just go and tidy myself up if I may.'

He nods curtly at me and turns to look out of the window. Mr Blackshaw cups my bottom beneath my skirt as I pass and I can't hold back the little yelp as his hand touches my inflamed skin.

His Lordship's eyebrows climb to his hairline as he

regards me with bewilderment. 'Everything all right, Mary?'

'Sorry, sir,' I say, flustered. 'It was just ... I pricked myself. With a hairpin.'

'Well, be careful,' he admonishes.

'Yes, do be careful, Mary,' echoes Mr Blackshaw. 'We don't want you doing yourself an injury.'

'No, sir. Sorry, sir. Excuse me, sir,' I babble, backing out of the music room.

Miss Lily is just making her way down the stairs as I close the door. She looks lovely and for a moment I can't believe she's the same girl who was in such a state earlier.

'Does my father suspect anything?'

'Not a thing,' I tell her. 'But next time perhaps you should find guests even farther away to send him to.'

She smiles slyly. 'Actually, I was thinking I might go and visit my cousin in the south of France. I couldn't go alone, of course. I should never be able to dress myself without my maid. And Father wouldn't want me to neglect my lessons either.'

I return her smile and reach out to stroke her creamy décolletage. She sighs sweetly.

'Perhaps Mr Blackshaw might teach us Latin next.'

Wanton Wagers
Morwenna Drake

'It's so delightful that you could make it for Christmas, Anne.'

'It was kind of you to invite me to Murton Hall, Aunt Sylvia,' Anne Pearson replied with a broad smile. Her aunt through marriage, Lady Sylvia Ellis was easy-going but with a sense of fun that complemented the Christmas festivities; just the person to lift Anne's spirits now that her period of mourning for her husband was over.

'I just couldn't bear the thought of you alone in that draughty house by yourself. And it's so dark up in Scotland.'

Anne laughed. 'No more than here in Somerset, Aunt, I promise you. It's not the hostile foreign clime you think it is.'

Her aunt wrinkled her nose in disagreement but didn't press the matter. Instead, she changed to another topic of which she disapproved. 'So, dear – when are you joining Dr and Mrs Morris?'

'Some time in February.'

'Anne, really – don't you think being a governess is beneath you? I mean, your uncle would see you taken care of – you don't need to –'

'Ah, but I want to, Aunt Sylvia,' Anne interrupted. Her aunt changed tack.

'Couldn't you be a governess for someone more –' She grappled for the right word.

'Respectable? Rich? No. Dr Morris and I get on well and I'm sure you would warm to him if you ever met him. Now, can we have an end to this discussion and a start to the festivities, please? You haven't introduced me to a single person yet – are you really that ashamed of your governess niece?' Anne's brown eyes twinkled mischievously.

'Of course not!' her aunt protested. 'And I see just the people now.' Sylvia guided her niece towards a tall woman whose slender figure verged on being gaunt. Her mousy hair was pulled back in a tight bun and, even though she was slightly shorter than Anne, she somehow managed to look down her nose at them as they approached.

Sylvia beamed at them. 'Miss Maitland? May I introduce my niece, Mrs Anne Pearson? I believe you were at school together.'

'Indeed,' said Anne. Her smile was just as cold and distant as Mary Maitland's.

'And I'm sure you remember Mr John Stanley, Frederick

54

Stanley's son? He's leaving us after Boxing Day to pursue a painter's life in Italy,' added Sylvia.

Anne turned her gaze to the young man. He boasted a smile that was a little too cocksure and a blue-eyed gaze that was too bold. His dark hair was slightly longer than was fashionable but it fell across his eyes in a rakish manner that was quite becoming. He gave a small bow.

'Of course I remember Anne,' he said smoothly. Such scandalous informality was not lost on Mary.

'We both remember you fondly, of course, Anne. But where is Mr Pearson this evening?' She emphasised his name and shot a sly glance at John. 'I very much wanted to meet him. He's a banker, isn't he? And I'm sure he'd be delighted to meet John as well, since he appears to be such a good friend of yours.'

Mary was enjoying herself immensely at the prospect of uncovering some scandal. As evenly as she could, Anne replied, 'My husband is dead, Miss Maitland. I am surprised that the purveyors of gossip upon which you so often rely did not mention such a fact to you.' Mary's mouth opened in genuine surprise, but Anne gave her no chance to reply. 'Now, pray excuse me. I feel the need for a glass of punch.'

Anne turned and walked away, anger boiling within her. Gossip didn't bother her – if it was accurate; bravo to the woman who cut you down with the truth, wrath to the woman who saw scandal in every shadow of a smile. She could hear Mary's voice, frantically squeaking an apology to Sylvia. Anne hoped her aunt was enjoying taking the high ground as much as she would have done.

Reaching the refreshments table, she paused to steady herself and someone offered her a full glass. She looked up to see John Stanley next to her.

'An impressive display, Mrs Pearson,' he said admiringly. She raised an eyebrow. 'Not "Anne" then?'

'Apologies, I was but teasing. I thought that our brief association as children might entitle me to such informality, but after the blow you dealt to Miss Maitland's pride, I'm not sure I want to risk your wrath.' His smile was cheeky, with a hint of something deeper. She found her memory thrown back to hazy summer afternoons when a group of them had gone to watch the haymaking. She had spent most of the time surreptitiously watching John's lithe form leaning against the fence with an easy smile beneath a straw hat. The hat was gone and the smile was more knowing now, yet she still felt that familiar twinge of excitement in his presence.

She straightened her back, refusing to be lost in foolish recollections. 'As I recall, our childhood association was me pushing you into the ditch after you tried to steal a kiss at the autumn ball, is that not so?'

'You cannot blame an innocent boy for trying his luck when such beauty is before him.' The compliment was delivered with a warm sincerity.

'I see your manners have improved, but I don't recall this "innocent boy" you speak of. I recall a scoundrel who had the heart of a poet and the devil's own love of gambling.' Her smile was saucier than it had been for a long time; it felt good on her lips.

John adopted an abashed look that didn't touch his twinkling eyes. 'Ah, it was not a poet's soul I turned out to possess, but that of a painter. But my love of gambling has never left me, I must admit. For example, I bet my father that within a year of being in Italy, I could be the most famous painter on the continent.'

A surprised laugh burst from Anne's lips. 'You jest?'

'Alas, only a little. I believe it was the most famous painter in England. But I cannot help myself when it comes to wagers. In fact, I have one for you, Anne.' She raised an eyebrow and waited. 'I'll wager you've not had a decent man between your legs since you were married.'

Despite her shock, Anne kept her face perfectly placid, but John grinned nonetheless. 'I'd even go so far as to say that you didn't have a good man between your legs when you were married. My recollection of Mr Pearson was an affable, elderly gentleman, fonder of port and cigars after dinner than the company of a nubile young wife. Am I correct?'

Anne couldn't tell if it was the twitch of her mouth or something else that gave away the truth, because his grin turned to a triumphant smile.

'That sounds like slander rather than a wager, Mr Stanley,' she said coldly.

'Then let me speak plainly. I bet even when you did indulge you rarely reached your own satisfaction. I bet you yearn to feel the heat of a man between your legs just once more before you are relegated to the school-room. And I bet I could satisfy that urge, if you would allow it, Mrs Pearson.'

Anne stood motionless. His comments cut too close to home. Stiffly she replied, 'You have been most diverting, Mr Stanley, thank you. But now I feel the need to seek less … provocative company.' She left with a small curtsey, hoping that her fluttering heart did not show in her gait. His words were shocking and accurate, and his offer unbelievably enticing. It was true that many nights she had lain cold and frustrated after her husband's visit, and that the thought of what she might be free to indulge in now her mourning was passed had not eluded her. And John Stanley, with his broad shoulders, slim waist and painter's fingers, was as intriguing a prospect now as he had been all those years ago.

Yet even the taint of scandal that soured such thoughts could not prevent her heart from leaping with excitement when a knock sounded on her bedroom door that night.

'Mr Stanley, this is most improper,' she hissed as he strode past her. She closed the door quickly, hoping no one had seen.

'I know.' He grinned wickedly. 'My valet has taken a

fancy to your maid and it suited both our purposes to find out when she finished her duties tonight.'

'What is it that you want?' she asked in exasperation, although she could guess.

'I have come about the bet we discussed earlier.'

'I see. And if I did have such carnal desires, what makes you think I would indulge them with you?' she asked haughtily.

'Because I bet I can make you orgasm while I remain fully clothed and without removing a single item of your own clothing.' She was intrigued. He stepped closer and against her better judgement Anne did not step away. 'And I bet I can stretch out your pleasure for an entire recitation of The Twelve Days of Christmas.'

Anne couldn't stop herself laughing, half amused, half shocked, thoroughly tempted. She glanced at his hands, imagining the feel of them running over her bare skin, and she had to hold back a shiver.

'My husband was adept with his fingers too, Mr Stanley,' she replied, one eyebrow cocked.

'I promise to keep my hands flat on the bed at all times. Interested?'

She was. With him standing before her in her own room, the threat of scandal seemed distant, merely a delightful frisson.

She smiled enticingly. 'We have a bet, sir, since I am guaranteed satisfaction either way.'

59

Her heart pounded as she allowed John to help her onto the bed. She expected him to lay her down but instead he made her kneel, facing the headboard, with her hands resting on it. She was shocked to see him lie down behind her and slide his head between her thighs, still fully clothed as promised.

'Are you ready Anne?' he asked from beneath her skirts. A conflicted, breathless laugh left her. The situation seemed ridiculous, yet every inch of her skin tingled with excitement.

'Ready and intrigued, John.'

'Then please begin your recitation.'

'On the first day of Christmas, my true love gave to me a partridge in a pear tree ...' Anne intoned and felt John's lips against her inner thigh; they warmed her flesh, moving upwards with purpose. By the third day of Christmas, he had reached the crease between her legs. She faltered at three French hens and John's voice came from below, his breath tickling her sex.

'Keep going, Anne. You've still nine days of pleasure to go.' He chuckled as his lips moved to her other leg, beginning down by her knee and working up again. Anne's legs quivered.

His lips moved much quicker on this side and she had reached the fifth day when his lips touched her own. Anne gasped as the warmth of his kiss spread upwards to form a tight knot in her belly.

'Five ... gold ... rings,' he prompted, each word punctuated by a kiss on her most intimate area. She shivered, arousal shooting through every limb.

'Five gold rings,' she repeated dutifully but breathlessly, 'four calling ... birds, three French hens ... two ...' She continued distractedly. John's kisses, so light against her legs, were now growing firmer. All her attention was between her thighs. As she spoke of seven swans a-swimming, his tongue speared down to her bud and her whole world contracted. Anne tried to concentrate on words she had recited dozens of times, but her mind kept slipping into a sea of pleasure where nothing existed but her own arousal.

Halfway through the tenth day of Christmas, John's lips fastened firmly onto her clitoris. Her husband had often done the same to her nipples but never with such effect. Anne squeezed her eyes shut, certain her legs would give way at any moment and she would tumble down onto his face. Her limbs were shaking and she could feel her climax drawing near.

As John's tongue lapped faster and harder against her, all recitation ceased and her breath came in ragged gasps. When orgasm bloomed within her, shaking her whole body with its force, a cry escaped her lips. She had never before given voice to such ecstasy and she collapsed, quivering, onto the bed.

As she lay gently panting, she was dimly aware that

John had moved to stand beside the bed. He leaned down and murmured in her ear, 'What a shame we only got to the tenth day. Perhaps I will have better luck with my bet tomorrow night.' He planted a gentle kiss on her temple. Sated for the first time in many years, Anne was already drifting into sleep as he left her room.

* * *

When Christmas Eve dawned, the sun crept over a crisp, frosty landscape. The horses in the stables flicked their tails. Servants scurried silently about their tasks.

Alone in her room, Anne turned away from a shaft of sunlight and buried her head, groggily wondering why she was so tired. Then, like a shock of cold water, memories of the night before returned.

She threw off the bedclothes, their weight suddenly suffocating. She hurried to the basin and pitcher that her maid had left but she stopped, her hands hovering over the water. She had expected to feel dirty, to feel the urgent need to wash away all traces of her shame. Yet she felt none of these things. Instead, she felt a tingling excitement and an unexpected smugness. She had certainly never experienced any such satisfaction with her late husband. John had introduced her to new possibilities and, rather than being horrified, she felt a craving to experience them again.

However the threat of scandal still soured her excitement and she did not seek out John's company that day. Yet in quiet moments she couldn't stop herself recalling the feel of his lips against her thighs, the warmth of his breath on her most intimate parts. She had to snap herself out of such reveries abruptly, fearing someone might read her sinful thoughts in her eyes.

As was customary, the whole household stayed up until midnight on Christmas Eve to welcome in Christmas Day, which would see the true start of the festivities. The adults drank wine and played cards, while the children sneaked back down in their nightclothes and were allowed to curl up by the fire to await the stroke of midnight.

At the appointed hour, a cheer was raised and the Yule log hauled onto the fire. Some of the more elderly guests retired but Anne was among those who stayed up to decorate the house with paper streamers, garlands of ivy and bunches of holly. She was tired but exhilarated and chatted enthusiastically to those around her. On the rare occasions when she permitted herself a glance at John, it was to find his eyes already on her. She was grateful for the weak candlelight so that no one could see the blush that coloured her face.

It was as she was indulging in such a glance that she felt a presence at her shoulder and was horrified to hear Mary Maitland's voice by her ear. 'He cuts quite a dashing figure, does he not?'

Anne concentrated hard on the garland of ivy she was hanging up. 'To whom do you refer?' she asked, trying to keep her voice light.

'Why, John Stanley, of course! You've been staring at him like a rabbit stares at a fox.'

The prospect of scandal drenched Mary's words. Anne glanced back again and her quick mind saw her salvation standing next to John. She stood straight, pulled her shoulders back and turned to face Mary with a cold, imperial look.

'I believe if you cast your eyes to the left of Mr Stanley you will see my uncle. If your eyes are keen, you will see the large glass of port in his hand. If your mind is sharp you will wonder, as I do, whether that is his fifth or sixth glass of the evening. And if you have any concern for your hostess, you will hope that he will not do anything to embarrass my aunt, as he did last Christmastide.' Mary's mouth opened and closed, working for words that would not come. In a cold voice Anne concluded, 'If you have been making eyes at another man over your husband's shoulder this evening, Mary, then that is your business. Please do not make it mine.' Anne walked sedately away from a stricken Mary. She felt so elated that, when she caught John's eye later that evening, she bestowed on him a saucy wink that he received with surprised pleasure.

Christmas Day itself was dark and drizzly, but nothing

could affect the cheer within Murton Hall. Presents were exchanged, carols sung and games played. By mid-morning, Anne felt as if she'd expended a whole day's worth of energy. She joined her aunt and her aunt's friends as they sat on the sidelines, watching the others dance or play cards. Even though she was hidden among the old spinsters and married women, her hand was solicited for several dances by different gentlemen, although not John. While she was grateful for this, since Mary Maitland watched her like a hawk, she nevertheless felt a twinge of disappointment. It wasn't until Boxing Day, his last day with them, when she saw him again.

It was late afternoon and the house was mostly empty. The ladies were resting in their rooms, the men were out at the Boxing Day hunt and the servants were snatching a moment's peace. Anne was lounging in an armchair in the library with her aunt, who was embroidering and passing on all the gossip. Anne listened while idly stroking her aunt's dog, a docile tan spaniel named Harry.

Sylvia was in full flow when the door opened and John walked in. Anne's heart quickened as he sauntered to the fireplace and leaned nonchalantly against it; she couldn't prevent her gaze travelling hungrily down his lithe form before she demurely turned her eyes away.

'Good afternoon, John – are you not at the hunt?' Sylvia enquired.

John smiled cheerily as he lit a cigar with a taper from

the fire. 'No, I leave tomorrow and I wanted to spend some time seeing to a few last matters.'

'Our best wishes go with you, my boy,' Sylvia said with fondness. 'You will be welcome here when you return from Italy – whether a year or ten years from now.'

'You are most gracious, madam,' said John, inclining his head.

During this exchange, Harry had abandoned Anne to sit at Sylvia's feet and look imploringly up at her. Sylvia patted him on the head.

'Yes, yes, Harry. It is well past time for our sojourn.' Sylvia got up then hesitated, glancing uncertainly between Anne and John.

'Do not worry about the lack of chaperone,' John said quickly. 'I came only seeking a light. I shall be returning to my room imminently to attend to some correspondence.'

Sylvia smiled and patted his arm on the way past. 'Such a good boy,' she said warmly. John hastened ahead and held the door open. Sylvia walked out, an excited spaniel bouncing around her feet, leaving Anne and John alone. John closed the door and quietly turned the key in the lock. The click of the mechanism set Anne's pulse jumping.

'What about your correspondence?' she asked as he sauntered over to the window.

'It can wait. Join me.' He held out a hand. Anne hesitated. Reason instructed her to unlock the door and walk away. A locked door itself would arouse suspicions, not to mention all the servants' secret passages. It was too risky.

Yet her heart was hammering with excitement, and reason was being silenced by a tingling anticipation. Her feet brought her to stand beside John. He had pulled the curtain almost shut so that, although Anne could view a small section of the garden, it was unlikely anyone could see in. As she peered through the gap, she felt John step up behind her. She straightened, pressing back against him, and a thrill of desire ran through her as his stiff manhood pressed against her buttocks.

'Do you have another bet for me then?' she asked, pleased that her voice sounded calm despite her inner turmoil.

'Indeed I do.' His breath warmed the back of her neck. Anne's mouth suddenly felt dry; she licked her lips.

'Do you see your aunt?' he asked. Anne nodded. Sylvia was heading away from them towards the rose garden. 'I bet I can make you come twice before she has finished her turn around the garden.'

Anne laughed and was forced to control the quaver in her voice as she said, 'You risk scandal, John. Can you not wait until –?'

'No, I cannot,' he said, urgency lending heat to his words. He reached down and tugged her skirt up to her hips before sliding his hand underneath. She gasped at his boldness even as she shuddered with pleasure. His fingers went straight for her sex, delving between the soft lips to find her bud. He chuckled at what he discovered, and the vibrations of his mirth rippled through Anne. 'And judging by how wet you are, Anne, I guess you cannot wait either.'

'John ...' Her words faltered as he began to rub her clitoris, spreading pleasure through her. Her hand reached for the wall as her knees weakened.

His other hand embraced her and plunged down her bodice so his fingers could tweak and tease her nipple. Anne closed her eyes and gave in to the sensations. Nothing existed beyond his finger slipping between her legs, his hand fondling her breast and his warm lips against her neck. Her climax came fast and unexpected, a torrent of sudden pleasure that left her panting.

John turned her slowly round to face him. 'That was once,' he observed with a wicked smile. She smiled, breathless and lost for words.

Gently pressing her against the wall, he began to plant feather-light kisses on the tops of her globes. Even as satisfaction cooled her blood, Anne felt lightheaded with rising desire again. John began to free her breasts but she stilled his hand.

'You must give a lady time to recover from your ... ministrations, John.' She gave him a wicked smile. 'And while I recover my breath, it would only be polite to allow me to explore you as you have explored me.'

As she spoke, her hands started to stroke down his chest, her fingertips tracing the contours of his muscles beneath his shirt. She wondered what it would be like to have his naked weight pressing down on her, their hot and eager flesh writhing as one, but knew it was not something she had leisure to discover today.

Her fingers deftly undid the buttons on his breeches as he bent his head to kiss her shoulder, his lips now as familiar on her skin as if they had been lovers for a lifetime. Anne wriggled her hand through the gap in his breeches until she found his manhood. It was thick and warm, twitching as her fingers brushed against it. She touched it gingerly, suddenly uncertain about such forwardness, but John's deep, lusty groan gave her heart, and she wrapped her hand around it. The heat of it stirred an answering glow within her and her sex tingled with anticipation.

A quick glance through the curtains revealed that her aunt was halfway through her turn about the garden; in the heat of the moment, the prospect of scandal only stoked her desire further. John's hands were beneath her skirt again and she parted her legs eagerly. He was pressed against her, his fingers slick upon her while her hand worked on his shaft, imagining it buried deep inside her. As if reading her thoughts, John removed his hand, freed himself and then, gripping her hips, guided himself inside her. He filled her in a way her husband never had and, for one delicious minute, they paused to stare into each other's eyes. Anne could feel every inch of him inside her and she could not resist the urge to wriggle against him, to feel herself stretch around his magnificent length.

He began to move his hips, sliding in and out of her with little grunts of effort as he supported her weight. She breathed his name against his cheek. 'It's never been like this. I never thought it could be.' She wrapped her legs around him, opening herself up to him body and soul.

John twisted his head to glance out of the window. 'I cannot see Lady Ellis. I fear we must bring this to a swift conclusion, my love.'

'By all means,' replied Anne breathlessly, uncertain whether she could have held off the orgasm that was rising within her even if Lady Sylvia Ellis herself had walked in on them. Her fingers grasped his coat, drawing them as close together as possible. John's thrusts became faster, more urgent, and Anne lost all sense of the world around her.

She urged him on with what little breath she had spare and her second climax flooded through her only a moment before his own. They cried out together as Anne rocked her hips against him, greedy for every last ounce of pleasure she could glean, until she thought she might faint from exhaustion and satisfaction.

In the wake of their pleasure, her legs still wrapped around him, she planted a tender kiss on his neck. He

70

returned it lovingly as he lowered her gently to the floor. Anne gritted her teeth against the shooting pins and needles in her feet but even that could not dislodge the smile from her face.

As they rearranged their clothes, silence stretched between them. Anne could think of no words that could do justice to her feelings but felt that something should be said before the silence turned sour. She commented, 'You won your bet, sir.'

John looked up, appearing both surprised and somewhat lost for words himself. Then he gave her that roguish smile of which she had become so fond.

'And yet I find the pleasure was not necessarily in the winning, but in the manner of it. And please – call me Johnny, when we are alone. All my most intimate friends do.'

'I fear that no such opportunities will present themselves if you are to leave tomorrow … Johnny.'

John was stepping forward with words on his lips when Sylvia's voice and footsteps echoed down the corridor. With a look of regret, John hurried to the door, unlocked it and waited behind it so that he could slip out unseen once Sylvia had entered.

'My dear!' Sylvia exclaimed when she saw Anne. 'Why are you next to the window on a chill day like today? Come sit by the fire.'

Glancing wistfully after John as he disappeared from

sight, Anne joined her aunt by the fire as she replied, 'Thank you for your concern, Aunt, but I assure you I am quite warmed through.'

* * *

John awoke several times during the night. He wanted to be away at dawn and, although his valet had promised faithfully to rouse him, he still woke repeatedly and checked his clock.

So he was more than surprised when he finally swung his legs out of bed, stretched, walked over to his dresser and found an envelope addressed to him that had not been there when he retired. He glanced at the door, wondering when his visitor had slipped in unnoticed. The delicate cologne surrounding the envelope conjured up one word: 'Anne'.

He held it a moment, staring at it thoughtfully with a mixture of hope and foreboding. When he eventually opened and read it through, he could honestly say it was not what he had been expected.

My dear Johnny,
I have so enjoyed our diversions together this Christmas. You have been a light in this widow's dark world and I thank you for it.
And now it seems only fair that I should place a

bet before you in return. I shall bet that in the course of your travels some young Italian heiress will dazzle you and that your natural charm and unique skills will soon win her hand in marriage. I would bet that, as a consequence of this, you will return in a haze of glory and happiness, and will not have a second glance for the dour governess of a country doctor.

But when you do return, seek me out. I shall be waiting to hear about your travels – and to see whether I have lost my bet.

Your fondest friend,

Anne Pearson

John read the missive through a second time to commit it to memory, then he placed it in the grate and set a match to it. He knew too well the scandal that would be caused if it was read by any other. It warmed him just to know she had written such words; he did not need to keep them. He smiled as he watched the paper blacken and curl. He had not even left for Italy yet and already he was counting the days until his return.

The Kiss
Ludivine Bonneur

I see his bare chest for the first time ever. The shock almost makes me drop the tray. He is sitting upon the edge of the bed, bending down to kiss and joke with Madame, who is propped up on the pillows as usual. His shirt is open, yet to be buttoned up. I have caught him dressing. I feel my cheeks go red and hurriedly put the tray down and scurry to attend to the shutters. I pull them back to let the June morning flood in, but then it's like I've done it on purpose just to get a clearer view of him. I can see my hands shaking. What if I had entered two minutes earlier, when his trousers were still to go on?

'Ah, Sidonie, *mon chouchou*,' he says to me as brightly as ever, 'how are you this lovely day?'

It makes me colour up even further to hear him use that term of endearment in front of Madame, but this has never bothered him. I had been unaware of the phrase when I first came here, and wondered how it could possibly be a good thing to be called a cabbage. The others told me, with some bitterness, that it meant 'favourite'. They thought I had asked just to ram it down their throats. Still now some of them sneer the name at me, saying, 'Here comes *le petit chou*' when I go in for lunch, or 'Pass the bread to The Master's Cabbage.' He also sometimes calls me his 'little peach', but I am careful not to make the same mistake and tell anyone this. I think it is because my cheeks are so red. He doesn't know they are only like this when he is around.

I sneak another look as I go to pour the coffee. I have my head bowed but I can't help snatching a glance. Madame has her hand up resting on his chest, her elegant pale fingers making his flesh look firm and tanned. I spot some grey hairs amongst the black, just as on his head. This is only to be expected on a man older than my father. Monsieur celebrated his twenty-first birthday the very day the Blitzkrieg first came, so the story goes, which puts him at 49 now. Madame is maybe five years his junior and still as handsome as ever. She is so beautiful he doesn't even have a mistress in the city, or so they say. She looks flawless this morning, her hair so unruffled after a warm night that it must have been brushed, her skin showing traces of make-up without any smudging, suggesting it has been put on fresh today. She doesn't seem like the type to be so vain, but maybe I don't know her that well. She might sneak out of bed extra early to get herself ready, not wanting to look anything less than perfect in front of us servants. Or maybe it is just for him.

The belly looks firm, with no trace at all of fat around his middle, even though he likes his food. I can catch these glimpses because he is so untroubled by my presence with him thus. There is no insecurity. He stays as he was when I first entered, sitting there smiling down upon his wife, telling her that he is meeting the artist Duval in half an hour, which explains his early rising. Not, of course, that I'm supposed to be listening to his conversation. It is hard to turn a deaf ear to anything he says. His voice is so mellow and gentle, so deep and never angry. I wish it was my hand on his chest now, feeling that unflappable heart beating beneath.

I can catch theses glimpses because I am doing my duty as always, my regime set in stone. Each weekend they lie in, so I take them coffee and the paper at eight on the dot, knocking twice before entering, setting down the tray and opening the shutters to the balcony, then pouring the coffee and handing it to them in turn, Madame first. I then lay out their gowns at the foot of the bed, and take out fresh towels from the drawer to replace the ones from the previous night. These things I have done for over a year now, so I can almost do them blind, which means I can sneak just one more look at Monsieur with his shirt unbuttoned. Then I spoil it by spilling some coffee through not paying attention while pouring it. I give a little gasp of mortification, especially as it must be obvious where my eyes have been. I deserve chastisement but they are both smiling, almost knowingly, and Monsieur tells me, 'Never mind, my little cabbage.' They are so perfect. He is so perfect.

I don't know how I've held this job down. I get in such a state around him. He rises from the bed and slowly buttons up his shirt. It is of crisp white cotton and fits close to his skin. He never needs a jacket to hide unsightly bulges. All his clothes are tailored to fit exactly, all cut from the finest cloth. It would be heaven merely to lie against him and just stroke the soft material and feel the gentle warmth of his body beneath. If I were Madame I would do that every day. I'm staring again. I drag myself over to the robe, just about remembering that Madame will still need her gown even if he doesn't. I lay it out at the foot of the bed. It means passing near him again, turning my back on him, bending slightly over the bed as I spread the gown out. I am almost willing the pressure at my back from his hand to keep me there, to push me further towards the sheets.

There would be nothing I could do about it. He is, after all, my Master. His rights extend to everything in this household, including me. At my interview, Bernard, the *majordome*, made one thing implicitly clear: I was to do whatever the Master said or asked, immediately and without question, anything and everything.

'Forget all the nonsense talk of Marxism and revolution, of abolishing our class society. Instead, always remember how lucky you are,' Bernard had said. 'Monsieur gives us everything: a room of our own in the chateau in these glorious surroundings, food to eat from his farms, even wine from his cellar, all free. It costs us nothing to live and yet he *pays* us to be here. We want for nothing and yet he rewards us nonetheless. All he asks in return is that we clean a few rooms for him, take him his coffee, attend to his guests. The least any of us can do is anything he says.'

I try to remember this when I'm up at five to get the eggs in, but Bernard has a point. Our days are long and the work can be arduous, but it is done in good humour, we are treated very well and we get to sample some of the luxury of chateau life. Yes, it is borrowed luxury, but it has let me experience things way beyond my expectations. 'Servant' might be a dirty word in a country once again teetering on the edge of revolution, but Monsieur only owns my heart and soul because I want to give it. Equality would not let me have him any more than I can now; it merely robs me of my obligations to my Master. I *want* him to own me. I want him to order me to do the kind of things I do not possess the tongue to ask for myself.

He need only say the word now and I would have to go over. Maybe he would unclip my hair so it might spread across my face to cover my shame in front of Madame. The skirt of my outfit is short and loose. There is nothing to stop it being lifted with little more than a flick of the wrist. I wear no hosiery. We used to wear Lycra tights, added by Bernard to our uniform in concession to our constant pleading for shorter hemlines. Now they have been made optional by the Master, such is the summer heat. My horrible nylon panties would hopefully be down in a second, no doubt leaving the usual unsightly red line around my waist. Why aren't I wearing the beautiful silk ones I saved up to buy? He would order me to rise up to meet him and I would have to comply. I would feel the grasp of his strong hands on my hips, steadying me for his slide. Then he would be there inside me, driving deep until his body met with mine.

The country boys I came here to escape are said to do it like animals. They rut and hump and grunt, slapping your backside and calling you 'whore', even though they have no intention of paying for it. He would be more measured. It would be a slow, surging forward drive and a sliding exit, deep but controlled, building the heat within. He would be listening for my sighs, responding to them, ensuring I took my pleasure even though the act was supposedly only meant to be for his. Maybe he would plunder me with a little more harshness than he would Madame, just as a sign to her that I was merely a servant to be used in this way. Still, there would be no frantic impersonality from him. His instinct for chivalry would not allow it. There would be something like tenderness. He would bend forward so that I could feel the closeness of him, the press of his chest on my back, his breath in my ear.

Beneath my cheek and palms I would feel the satin of the bed sheets. My God, those sheets! When I first came here I thought them the epitome of rich snobbery, an expense just for the sake of it. Then I got to touch them, to feel them on my bare skin. I realised why you would never sleep on anything else if you could. I am the one now responsible for this room. I get to change the sheets. I can spend a long time smoothing them out, getting them as flat as possible, just to feel the tingling silkiness on my palm. I wondered what that sheer contact would feel like on other parts of my bare body, what Madame feels when she pulls up her nightdress.

It got the better of me one day. I knew they were both in the city and Bernard was in the wine cellar. I would not be disturbed. I have been told it is different elsewhere in Europe but here we strictly respect someone's privacy. Doors are kept closed and we do not enter any rooms without express purpose or direct invitation. This goes for the largest chateau as well as the smallest hovel. Over half the rooms in this house I have never entered and never will. There are rooms the Master himself has never stepped inside, even rooms that Bernard has not been in, and he is in charge of the running of the house. Since this is my room to clean, no other maid ever comes here. So I took off my dress. The sheets were to be cleaned anyway so it wouldn't matter. I slid in between them and lay there, in his bed. I felt down for signs of their shared desire, but there were none. Then, I'm a little ashamed to say, my panties came down too.

It is hard to describe the bliss of this material against your skin, rucking up in your own creases as you writhe. Only the fur of Madame's winter scarves comes close. I shivered whilst I did it, but it was a beautiful shiver. I shook from the dread of his premature return but my head was filled with the idea of him discovering me there in such a way. On a handful of occasions, maybe ten or more, I have had the sheets off the bed and gathered up before it gets too much for me. I find myself clutching the bundle, wrapping it into a tighter sausage to give it more substance. Somehow I end up face down on the bed, the bundle of sheets beneath me, embracing it tightly with arms and legs. Somehow I end up with my panties down and my bareness rubbing against the satin. The humiliation of being found humping the sheets almost makes me sob, yet still I would not postpone the day he comes in unexpectedly and finds me there.

It would indeed be a surprise. Except for bringing the

morning tray and when I have been expressly summoned by the bell, I am banned from even going to their room at a time when either of them might be present. In return, they know when I am likely to be cleaning the room and ensure they stay away. It could never happen by accident. For him to get me here alone he would have to order it. That is all it would take: one simple order, and I would have to obey. Maybe I shouldn't even expect any warning. Perhaps just a hand on my back to hold me down and the sound of his zipper coming open to announce he was to use me as he saw fit.

Imagine being entered whenever it took his fancy, without foreplay or so much as a by your leave, of just being laid out and stripped for his purpose. Is this all the treatment I can expect, even in these days of feminism and supposed equality? Imagine being used in front of his wife, in front of guests, of being done in the secret garden or in the stables, at any time of the day, just on his whim, without any power to refuse it. Fortunately when he is around it is never long before I am ready for him. Would he expect to finish inside me? Thanks to Monsieur Neuwirth contraception was legalised last year, although we are supposed to be a good Catholic country. Some of us are yet to embrace this new freedom but would he assume I had, simply because he was in his right to use me as it pleased him? It might not even occur to him that he has a need to withdraw.

It might save me some pain, at least. Before the pill, and I'm sure even now, another common method existed to avoid having the sin of premarital sex revealed by an unwanted pregnancy. As my friend Gabrielle once explained it to me:

'You have two holes down there. One is for the start and one is for the finish. The first is for pleasure, the second for relief,' the relief being his, in the form of a climax, and yours in the form of an ejaculation without conception.

Trouble was, or so the rumours went, most of those rural guys saw us country girls as pigs, and many didn't even bother with the first hole, going directly to the second. I wonder if Monsieur would commit such a rude act? Imagine being filled to bursting from the rear. Perhaps it is the only way he thinks to take us servants, not wanting to treat us as Madame's equal? God, what if she used her fingers inside me while he went at my behind! How could I stop them? The rich can do whatever they like so why would it surprise me to have them use me together? They are usually so nice to us all but behind closed doors must surely be a different matter.

Sometimes it shocks me when I hear what people get up to in this age of Free Love. I feel I should embrace it but I just do not have the nerve. The revolutionaries say the rich and authoritarian are morally devoid, but they only want to overthrow them to have a taste of that immorality themselves. Some of us can't do with the freedom; we need to be told, or made. I could choose a hundred guys from the street and find that none of them match the expectations of my fantasy. Then what? With Monsieur I simply know, since such skills and attitudes are born within him. You need only look at the beauty and happiness of his wife to see this is true. Force or otherwise, at least I would know I could not be taken by a better man. I stay leant across the bed for longer than is necessary but with his hand not pushing at my back there is nothing to do but straighten up and go off to the bathroom to swap their towels. In my absence I hear him bid Madame a cheery *au revoir*, and my heart sinks a little.

* * *

I cannot necessarily expect to see him again this day, at least not until the evening. Yet he calls for me unexpectedly, not an hour after he left the room. I am summoned to one of the private salons on the third floor. I have been to it a couple of times before with items for storage. It was almost empty then, with the carpet recently pulled up to leave a wooden floor. There is not much more to it now. Everything in it is white from the streaming sunlight and the sheets draped over all the furniture. The only things left uncovered are Madame's old dressing screen in one corner and a large cheval mirror standing near the centre of the room. My Master is standing there in only his dressing gown – the silk one with the Japanese design. I do not know what he has beneath it but I can see a V of exposed flesh at his chest and his bare legs are testament to the fact he has no pyjama bottoms on. Why he is like this I have no idea, but I can feel the heat in my cheeks. I get a sudden mental flash of him opening the gown to reveal his nudity beneath.

However, such images must wait because he is not there alone. He is with Monsieur Duval, the artist. The latter has a sneer and a large mole on his face, neither of which I am particularly partial to. Perhaps I'm being unkind and judging him based on what Bernard has said. Bernard does not like M. Duval one bit. He scorns him for being 'jumped-up nobility', that is, one whose ancestors were ennobled during Bonaparte's time, usually for nothing more than holding clerking duties. The Master's family have held their title for centuries. They have owned these same lands, raised armies at their own expense that fought for kings and emperors and even republics. For Bernard that means everything. He thinks breeding and class are innate. He cannot bear the fact that our Master is considered no more than bourgeois these days, when his blood is so noble. The others tease him and remind him that nobility means nothing in our country any more, that class was something the government wanted to abolish once and for all. This infuriates Bernard, who is funny about such things. I remember how angry he was once when a visiting Englishman referred to him as a valet, rather than a *majordome* – a mere gentleman's assistant rather than the overseer of an entire estate.

'It's not like they don't have butlers over there!' he had shouted in his fury.

For him it was not a slight on his own position but on his Master's, as if Monsieur was just one of the postwar *nouveau riche* industrialists rather than the current Lord of an ancient line. It was only the old nobility that understood the values, that innately appreciated fine art and literature and wine, that grasped the finer technicalities of warfare. In short it was only they that could keep our country great.

'Monsieur has more breeding in his little finger than Duval has in his whole body!' Bernard had said.

Of course it didn't help that Duval had thrown off his supposed nobility and become a communist. Bernard was not fond of communists, and maybe he had a point. My Master might still be the same man without his grand estate, but he wouldn't look so beautiful without his grooming, or his expensive clothes and shoes. Why rob the state of that beauty just out of jealousy? There would be no call for his refinement and chivalry, since such things would be regarded as snobbish. Servants would no longer exist, so there would be none to demonstrate his uncommon decency towards us. It is his respect for all that I admire most, his instinct for how best to treat everyone from royalty to lowly peasants. I wouldn't have to tell him he could be a little rougher and ruder with me than he might be with his more refined conquests, because girls today have more freedom of spirit and fire in their bellies.

'Sidonie, I wish to ask something of you,' my Master says, and that fire in my belly ignites. This is the first time he has used such a phrase outside my own imagination. Whatever he now commands I must obey; my status forbids me to refuse him. I am nervous of having to do things in front of the much less attractive Monsieur Duval. Maybe that's what the rich like to do: share their spoils. There are enough rumours among the girls of what goes on in the circles of the wealthy, although none of us can actually claim to have seen any such things going on here at the chateau. But they must. The rich can do whatever they want, so why wouldn't they?

The Master is telling me something but I cannot really concentrate because I'm wondering what he will have me do on the large trunk that has been positioned in the centre of the room. It has been covered by an old bed sheet but one end has not dropped down as intended and I can see and identify the trunk beneath. I can also see that a duvet has been laid over the trunk too, no doubt to act as padding. The cheval mirror is set to the rear and one side to reflect all of this, a blatant sign of their rude intentions that makes my blood fizz. I realise the Master is awaiting some sign that I understand his request.

I have to drag his words back to mind and formulate them, just to know what he is asking of me. It seems Duval has been commissioned to paint a portrait of Madame and Monsieur. It had to be Duval, according to my Master, because he is such a brilliant artist. No one else would have done. However, Duval does not like to do traditional works and has only agreed to do so if he can also paint a second portrait in his preferred style. I'm not sure what any of this has to do with them putting me over the covered trunk, and frankly the wait to discover my fate is not doing my racing heart much good. Perhaps I am to be payment for Duval's efforts? I look blankly at my Master, but surely convey that I am at his disposal whatever he chooses to command of me.

'The trouble is,' says the Master with a smile of apology, 'Madame will not sit for this second portrait, not just because of time constraints, but because of the manner in which my good friend here wishes to capture us.'

The artist raises his eyebrows and tuts with exasperation. There is more hesitant explanation from the Master before the artist rudely interrupts.

'Madame refuses to sit for the portrait today because

I require her to be nude. This is despite the fact that the composition was conceived purely with her in mind. Presumably she thinks herself above such things.'

'Most of the time you will be covered with a gown,' says the Master hurriedly, 'but Monsieur Duval cannot paint from imagination alone ...'

'Of course I can't,' snaps Duval. 'What artist can?'

So that is it. The Master wishes to lure me out of my clothes by using me as an artist's model. It is a subtle trick. First they get me naked and alone, and then they have their wicked way. Monsieur tells me he was prepared to try to find a substitute from outside but I am so much like Madame, in stature as well as in looks. Even then he would not have asked, he tells me, but having caught him in a state of undress this morning, and having acted with such decorum about it, I was suddenly deemed the ideal replacement. How clever for him to have been bare-chested when I came in this morning, just to provide this excuse. I will be paid extra for my efforts, I am told. Arrangements can be made to cover my duties in my absence. No one else will be told precise details of what I am to do, in order to protect my modesty. The final portrait will hang in the master suite, so no other, apart from Madame and Monsieur – and my good self, as maid of the room – will ever see it; another reason it has to be me.

'I will need to sit with you for most,' says the Master,

'but if you prefer, whilst you are to be unclothed I can be absent, or I could summon another servant to take my place.'

'Sir, if I am to be nude,' I say with some passion, 'I would prefer to be so in front of a man of status and grace, and not some gossiping groom. And I most definitely prefer not to be left alone with some stranger!'

Duval looks a little affronted but my Master is more worried about the unintended slight given to me. His sheepish look is enough to pacify me.

'So, you agree then?' Monsieur says.

How could I not?

* * *

I am required only for the day. Madame had sat for a previous session, in which she could remain fully clothed, so that Duval could do the background and roughly sketch in the foreground. I am needed as he fleshes out his subjects. I am needed because I am too lowly to refuse to strip. The Master will get me bare and ravish me, claiming I remind him too much of his wife when she was also twenty, and he will do all those rude things they do today which he had missed doing to her when they were both young. To ensure I don't have second thoughts and run, they gave me only the time it takes for Duval to uncover his easel and set out his paints.

Monsieur has provided me with one of Madame's satin gowns, which I find hanging behind the screen. It is almost as if he knows I cannot resist when I feel that silkiness against my skin.

Monsieur is already sat upon the covered trunk when I bashfully emerge. He holds out his hand and I go nervously towards him.

'Do you know of Rodin's sculpture commonly called *The Kiss*?' he asks me quietly. I nod, the butterflies alive in my belly. He tells me it is Madame's favourite work of art. It depicts the lovers Francesca and Paolo from Dante's *Inferno*, moments before they were discovered and slain by Francesca's jealous husband. It was Rodin's homage to women, to depict them as full equals in love to men. Duval's idea is to recreate this work, so emotive a theme in today's society, but in paint form. Madame and Monsieur are to be depicted in the pose of Rodin's doomed lovers, painted against a background of blue covered with recent examples of graffiti taken from the walls of Paris buildings, daubed by the students and strikers. He is to use phrases like 'we will have good masters when everyone is their own' and 'the golden age was when gold didn't reign'. Apparently Duval thinks it highly comical to capture his noble friends at the very moment they teeter on the edge of losing it all in this current uprising.

'He also thinks it amusing,' the Master whispers

conspiratorially to me, 'to paint a portrait in which you can barely make out the subjects' faces!'

Our closeness is making my heart thump. I'm sure he must be able to hear it. If you do not know this sculpture then be aware that I am obliged to sit very near to him, between his open thighs, leaning almost against him with my right shoulder. My left arm is up, the hand around his neck, as if I am desperately pulling him down for our final kiss. His right hand rests just below my left hip, the one facing the artist. It barely touches me at all, almost hovering, and yet imagine later when this hip is bare, when his large hand is on my naked flesh. When that time comes my breasts will be fully exposed, particularly the left one. My bottom will be less so, pressed as it is to the trunk, which Duval will presumably paint like the stone of the original. However, a quick glance round shows me that it is actually more visible to both men present, reflected as it is in the cheval mirror behind me. So that's what it was for, those devious devils!

It takes less time than I envisaged to get into the correct pose. We have a postcard of the original to refer to, plus brusque instructions from M. Duval. My face reddens when I realise that my thighs are not to be squashed together, hiding all. The left knee points down and only time will tell how much of me this will reveal. Having leant into him it is almost automatic to reach around for his neck to help my balance, and that in turn automatically pulls him in. There is a brief pause as we look into each other's eyes, both aware of what is to happen next, although I can only guess at what this will lead to. Then my head sinks lower towards his shoulder and I hold my breath in readiness for the soft contact of his lips. I close my eyes, only for them to spring immediately open as Duval calls out,

'That's it! Hold still – don't move!'

We freeze, our mouths less than an inch apart, open, expectant. Now he can surely hear my heart. I can feel his gentle breath, smell the fine fragrance at his neck. His other hand, the one not on my thigh, is down behind me, not holding me. This means my grip around his neck is nearly all I have to keep me in position. It suddenly strikes me that we are hardly touching at all, despite such close proximity. If I didn't suspect his intentions otherwise, I would say he only allowed me to replace his wife because of this fact. He has humour in his eyes. It is difficult not to melt into him but even the slightest movement has Duval barking his annoyance and telling me to hold still. Monsieur gives me a little smile at this latest rebuke. If I stuck out my tongue I could trace it across his lips. He knows he has the right to my body and this closeness is just torture.

For ages we hold like this, my head angled away so that I cannot even see straight into his eyes. He whispers the tale of Dante's lovers to me in full and I feel every ounce of Francesca's pain at her forbidden love for Paolo. We have to break every once in a while as I simply cannot maintain the position. Duval uses the time to march around chattering to himself about how he should have got a professional model in, and Monsieur simply smiles and uses the time to talk softly to me. We stay close even in these breaks. I can see all his perfections – the completely smooth skin of his chin and jaw, despite the harsh dark hair that will grow there incessantly; the neatly precise grooming of his sideburns and eyebrows; the lack of wiry hair sprouting from nostril and ear that both Bernard and Duval sport.

All morning we are like this, most of it just an inch apart. It is almost like wearing him, but agonisingly it is not quite close enough. We talk back and forth, since there is nothing else to do.

'Stop laughing!' Duval cries out impatiently.

I wish Duval would go up in a puff of smoke and leave the two of us alone.

Bernard told me never to speak unless spoken to by my Master, and yet here I am doing exactly that. He is disarming and very engaging. I know exactly why Madame loves her beautiful husband so fiercely. It takes everything to stop myself dragging him in that last inch. I cannot wait for the moment Duval finally wants to paint our kiss and tells us to press our lips together.

'Lunch!' cries the artist, setting down his brush and

striding out, as if even a second's procrastination would ruin his appetite. We are alone, almost frozen into our near embrace. I think this might be the time he acts, but he gently puts his arm around my back, rights me and slowly draws away. He could take advantage of me now, since no one would enter and disturb him, but I remember the convenience of my nudity that the afternoon session will bring. Then the animal will come out and he will have me all over this room, maybe even dragging me off to his own bed in his passion. He rises and tells me he will fetch me something to eat, the Master serving the maid. We break for an hour, eating together, sitting as equals just like the revolutionaries would have us, except they do not realise what they would steal from the world, from me. I do not want the common touch. I want to be taken by nobility. It is the authority of his bearing, his sophistication and his wealth that make me always so ready for him.

'Begin!' commands Duval, sweeping back into the room, and we smile at each other and slide back into position, so practised now. My heart begins to beat faster again, although the trepidation about removing my gown in his presence has all but gone.

'Gowns off!' cries Duval.

Neither of us complies immediately. I see him looking down at me, though I cannot make out the expression. Then his hand lifts from my hip and I can feel him undoing the belt of his gown. I hear the sweep of silk over his firm body and the garment drops away from his shoulders. I hear him grasp it and slide it out and drop it in a heap on the floor. His legs are splayed so there can be no hiding it. One look down and I would see him in all his glory, except of course that my view is blocked by his face and by my own chest and raised thigh. I can just about make out a portion of his firm torso and his muscular left shoulder and bicep. It is not much considering he is totally naked, in brilliant sunlight, just inches from me. I wonder what he looks like down there, whether he already has a swell from the rude intentions he must have towards me. I imagine he is too controlled to be like this in front of his friend. I realise he will almost certainly wait until we are alone to act, and that thought sends a tingle of joy all over my body.

'Mademoiselle?' says Duval, impatient that I am yet to strip. I think I could but my arm is so stiff from being in the one position that it has almost seized up. Monsieur mistakes my hesitation for reticence. Slowly, patiently he reaches to my middle and unties the single bow that keeps my gown in place. He begins to slide the gown off my shoulders, keeping his eyes on mine. I have to straighten up and drop my arm to allow the gown to slip off. I feel the slight coolness on my skin, the hairs on my body already raised. My breasts are bare but his eyes never leave mine. He tugs at the gown and it comes free, to be dropped on the floor alongside his. There is coolness at my exposed crotch and I bite my bottom lip, suddenly aware that the sensation is caused by dampness between my open thighs.

My cheeks are aflame. He sees this and says, 'Do not worry, Little Peach, I can see nothing.'

He could easily look down and see me, but it seems he is too well-mannered to do so. The strange thing is I wish he would. It might instigate those passions he has so far chivalrously kept in check. I'm sure it is a thin line between restraint and losing control. I know it is a battle I fear I am losing.

'What can he see in the mirror?' I ask my Master, knowing it will mean looking there, seeing the reflection of my rear. He glances over, holds there as he catches sight of my young rump, then blinks a couple of times before looking away.

'The mirror is to divert the sunlight so he can paint us as if lit from behind and not from the side, that is all,' he says.

I wonder if he felt a swell down there at the sight of me, a stirring to awake the ardour. Now we are naked it is even harder to stay this close without gathering him in for a full embrace. Everything about me seems to be reaching out for him – my lips, the hairs on my limbs all up on end. Even the little points of my breasts have stiffened, whether from nervousness or desire I know not.

I am aching for the closer contact. It seems he must lose the battle and fall into me at any second. I picture him growing down below, his mind as full of naughty images as mine is. I can almost feel the heat of his swell on my thigh. Soon it will fill out completely and touch me. I dare not move and break the spell. The talk has dried up because of our nudity and because we are hanging on the point of giving in to immorality. Yet still he does not take me.

'Monsieur,' I whisper, 'if it helps our artist I would not consider it too bold a move on your part to kiss me. For the sake of reality, I mean.'

'Ah, my Little Cabbage, that's the thing,' he replies. 'In Rodin's sculpture their lips do not meet. It suggests they were taken from each other the moment before they could seal their love. It is what makes their one and only embrace so poignant.'

I feel my stomach tighten. These hours since lunch I have stayed frozen, totally captivated by him, the heat ever building between my legs. I have sat completely naked, resigned to be used by him, desperate for that first contact, the kiss that would break the seal and unravel our passions. Now the afternoon is slipping away and it seems the kiss will not be ordered after all, despite everything. I have been there for the taking but he has not done so. I have been naked and yet he has kept his gaze steadfastly away from my body. His hand has not slipped from my hip and down between my thighs, even though he must feel the heat coming from between them and smell the readiness as I can. He has not pulled me into him, crushing his lips to mine, made my tongue swirl with his. He has not forced me onto his lap, my legs wrapped around his waist, his hands grasping and squeezing my behind, his fingers sliding into me from the rear. He has not given in to his lusts and stood up upon the trunk, grown right before my eyes, gripped my hair and then forced himself into my mouth.

None of this he has done, despite my expectations, despite my hopes. It suddenly strikes me that he is not going to do so either. He is too much the gentleman. The very attributes I love him for will see me denied. Even though we have been so close in broad daylight, his respect for me means that, if he just closed his eyes now, I could regain my gown and put it on and slip away without him seeing any more of me then that little portion of my rear, and even then he quickly averted his eyes. As incredible as it seems, I have been naked and closer and more ready for this man than any other in my life, a man who clearly finds me attractive, and yet still I will be allowed to go without him fucking me.

'*Voilà!*' cries Duval, shaking me out of my trance. He is off out of the salon without even a goodbye, closing the door behind him loudly. I see he has tidied away his paints whilst I have been distracted. I can only presume the painting is finished and that is that. I look back at my Master, still only inches away. My tired neck can now straighten. I can look directly into his lovely eyes. I still see humour there, not mischief. We are naked and all alone and he has the right to do whatever dirty things he wants to do to me, yet still he is not going to bend me over this trunk and stuff me full. I feel pressure on my hand from his head. He is trying to ease himself back so that we are not so perilously close to kissing. I resist. I no longer care about immorality or what giving into it does to my soul. I sink forward and kiss him, full on the lips. My tongue tries to find his but meets with reticence. His hands do not grip my behind as I imagined, but instead go up to my arms to gently prise me away. The contact is lost but I still hold him as close as before.

'Sidonie, I am married!' he says, entreating me.

'I will not tell,' I say. 'Every gentleman has a mistress.'

'But I love her,' he says, still quietly. 'She is all I will ever need.'

Again my stomach turns cartwheels. I hadn't thought his chivalry and devotion to be that deeply ingrained. He truly is a man amongst men, not that this helps me. There is no way I can let this moment pass. What is the point of equality and sexual freedom if you cannot take what you need? I rise up onto my knees on the trunk, still with my hand tight against the back of his neck. I push my little titties out into his face. He is aghast and his still parted lips allow me to push one swollen nipple home. I force it in, trying to fill his mouth with my soft breast, pulling his head towards me. My other hand reaches down and I grasp his prick, feeling the delicious weight and warmth of it in my palm, the automatic swell against my gripping fingers. He twists his head to free his mouth of my breast and I sense the instant cool of his saliva upon my skin. His cock cannot help but harden and any second he will give in.

'Stop it, Sidonie!' he cries. 'I cannot do this!'

My hand is already working on him down below, gliding up and down his fattening length to defeat his resistance. He grips my wrist and pulls, dragging me off bit by bit although I am determined to hold him. His strength is too much and my arm is forced up and outwards, as if he is trying to unbalance me and throw me off the trunk. I shuffle sideways, my feet on the trunk now, thinking I should leap clear, but as I turn away my wantonness takes over again. I no longer have a hold of him. I shuffle further round so that my back is at his face, seemingly ready to dismount. Then I bring my weight down upon him, sitting hard on his lap.

I spit myself upon him and it slides all the way up inside me. I am far too ready to do anything but open up. The penetration is shocking and electric, and searingly wonderful. I hear his throaty gasp beneath my own squeals. Now he must yield. Before he can react I have forced my ankles beneath his thighs so I can grip him with my legs and prevent him lifting me clear. Just being full of him is making me whimper and quake. I need to feel his passion too. I move up and down, drawing more breathless gasps from him. I rise up and slap down hard. I can feel my desire pouring out to drench him.

He is still beseeching me to stop. He tries to drag me off but I grip tighter with my thighs and ankles, locking me in position. I feel his fingers all over me, gripping, pinching, slapping – trying anything to prevent me milking the pleasure from his loins. In the end he can do nothing but wrap his arms up underneath mine and grasp my shoulders, pulling downwards so that my riding motion is arrested. I cannot go up and down but I can go back and forward so I do, grinding out more pleasure. He has no other way to resist me. I see his face reflected in the mirror, the shock and defeat in his eyes, mixed with lust. I slide back and forth, saturated now. I squeeze my little swollen titties while he watches in the mirror. The sight of my rudeness ensures he stays hard within me, despite his pleas for me to stop. My right hand drops down to my groin and I rub myself, immediately drawing out the unstoppable rush of bliss. I have my eyes closed but I know he is watching me. I am saying over and over, 'Fuck me, fuck me, fuck me,' grinding against him, frigging myself, being more free and wanton than I had ever dreamed possible.

He will not be able to climax but nothing can stop me. I do so with racking force, falling back against him, my hips jerking, my chest thumping. He is the motionless organ of my pleasure, resigned with his usual grace to sacrificing his principles for the good of others. His arms drop down and release the pressure at my shoulders now that I am done. He is still hard inside me and it seems a sin to leave him this way. My pleasure has been taken but my mind won't clear of lust. I slide off him, releasing my grip on his legs. I should climb off and accept whatever fate awaits me but I don't. Instead I go on all fours, my rear thrust out at him, inviting him to take me any way he fancies, as is his right.

Odd, despite my overpowering desire, part of me wants him to refuse me, since staying true to his wife makes him even more of the man I hold in such high regard. If he does not enter and have me now then I am finished; cast out, no doubt, from his safety into a world I know nothing about, of rioting and graffiti and Molotov cocktails hurled at police. My only hope would be to join the revolutionaries I so despise, to try to beat them to the gates as they storm this chateau, and to ravish my peerless Monsieur a final time before they strip his nobility away. I feel his movement behind me and I pray that he cannot resist. So strange how I want all those principles I love and admire to desert him now.

The Lady and the Maid
Kathleen Tudor

Anna selected a necklace from her collection on the table and held it up. It was plucked neatly from her hand, and she savoured that tiny moment when Jane's fingers brushed against her own. Her maid had been with her since she was only a girl, and the maid was only the cook's daughter, and yet their touches had grown fewer and fewer over the years.

Jane slid the necklace around Anna's throat and fastened it, and Anna shifted in the mirror, admiring its hang with a critical eye. Her hair had already been dressed, styled into an updo that looked as if it might have required hours but had taken skilled Jane only a few minutes.

'Do you think I need another comb?' Anna asked, glancing at the collection she'd laid out for consideration.

'No, my Lady, unless you want to. I think it looks

lovely, so simple.' Jane backed away and Anna stood to turn in front of the full-length mirror.

'Yes, I suppose it does.' She nearly asked Jane how she looked, but the girl always gave the same flattering answer, and Anna had grown tired of the assurances. Anyway, Jane wouldn't let her go down to dinner looking like riffraff.

'Papa said he had something important to announce at dinner,' she said. 'I hope he's pleased with me.' She'd run over and over her list of possible transgressions but, try as she might, she wasn't sure what she might have done to attract her father's attention. He was always busy with some aspect or other of the estate, and she tried to stay out of his way.

'I'm sure it's something nice,' Jane said. She tilted her head enquiringly and Anna waved a hand.

'You may go. Thank you, Jane.'

Jane bobbed one final curtsey and vanished.

* * *

Anna picked at her tiny portion of roast and resisted the urge to fidget. Her father had yet to tell her whatever it was he wanted to say, and he and her mother chattered amiably with her grandmother and her cousin Lady Frances.

She picked up her wine and took a tiny sip, then

went back to picking at her dinner. Her mother glared subtly and raised her eyebrow, and Anna sat up straighter and smiled, pretending engagement with the insipid conversation. *Really!*

She was just beginning to wonder if she could get away with excusing herself with a 'headache' or some such fabrication when her father cleared his throat and turned towards her. 'My dear, you've been very silent tonight.'

'My mind has been wholly occupied with wondering what you might wish to discuss with me tonight, Papa,' she said. She saw her mother turn and glare at her again, but only smiled even more sweetly and said, 'Perhaps you might put my curiosity to rest?'

'Yes, well, I had thought to wait until we'd all gone through for tea, but I suppose now is as good a time as ever.' He adjusted himself in his seat in an unconscious movement that she recognised as 'putting on his Earl countenance'. She sighed at the apparent gravity of the conversation, but made an effort to keep her frustration to herself, lest her mother feel the need for further reprimand.

'Well, my dear, since you may not inherit this estate, and are well beyond a minimum marriageable age –'

'Darling,' her mother interrupted, her tone warning. A good thing, because Anna was fit to burst over the comment herself.

'Well, she is,' the Earl muttered. 'My dear Anna, we

feel that it is time for you to marry. We shall be inviting several likely gentlemen to dinner over the next few months, but I promise you, Anna, if you refuse to choose one, then one of them will be chosen for you. Even if you don't want to marry your cousin Charles to become countess, you must consider your future, and I wish to see you settled.'

Frances and Grandmother had fallen completely silent as they regarded Anna, no doubt waiting to see if she would throw one of her legendary tantrums, but Anna was too stunned to speak. She knew in her heart that she would have to marry one day, but she wasn't ready! None of the eligible men she could think of were the least bit interesting to her, especially dim, foppish Charlie. Couldn't they see that she simply needed more *time*?

She pushed back her chair, waiting until she felt slightly less dizzy before she stood. Papa hastened to rise as well, and she turned towards him. 'If you will excuse me, I feel I am not at all well. I'm going to lie down.' She dipped her head respectfully in his direction, then spun and strode gracefully from the dining room.

Behind her she heard Papa sigh. 'I knew she would be like this. I had hoped having you here might keep her calmer, dear Frances. Perhaps you could talk to her about the joys of married life?'

Anna moved purposefully toward the stairs and into her bedroom and rang for Jane, but she didn't even wait for her maid before she started to tear the comb from her hair. She was wrestling with the clasp on her necklace when Jane arrived, hurried to her side, silently took the clasp and swiftly removed the necklace.

'Are you well, my Lady?' Jane asked.

Anna looked at her lovely maid in the crisp black and white uniform and sighed. 'My father thinks it's high time I married,' she said. 'He swears that if I can't settle on any of the gentlemen he presents me with, he'll choose one himself.' Jane remained silent, carefully not offering an opinion, and Anna stepped forward crossly, pushing herself out of the gown that Jane had nearly finished unbuttoning for her. 'Don't you have an opinion about anything?'

'Of course, my Lady, but it isn't for me to say,' she said. She bobbed a tiny curtsey and helped Anna into her nightdress and robe.

'No, I suppose it isn't.' Anna turned, surprising Jane. 'But I find myself wishing more and more that you would share one, anyway.' Jane smelled of soap and of lamb stew. Anna must have interrupted the servants' dinner when she'd rung for her. 'Are you going hungry on my account?' she asked. She was so close that she could feel Jane's breath lightly fanning the hairs that drifted around her head, freed from the comb but still untamed by a brushing.

'No, my Lady, they'll set me aside a portion of supper for when I return. But I wasn't that hungry anyway.'

Anna smiled sadly at the echo of her own lie. Her lovely maid, willing to go without, to serve her lady. Such loyalty and kindness were rare, she thought. And Jane was one of the kindest and best-spirited people she knew, or at least Anna thought so. A beautiful soul to go with a beautiful face. 'I wish I could choose to marry you over any of the English gentlemen,' she said, startling them both. Jane stepped back, and Anna turned and seated herself at the vanity to let Jane brush her hair out.

Where had such a thought come from? Certainly it was sinful and wicked for two women to marry, wasn't it? Such a ridiculous notion was so exceptional that it had never been mentioned. Perhaps it was a sin so wicked that no one dared speak of it. She could have laughed at that, but sorrow still lay heavy in her breast.

Jane picked up Anna's brush and started to run it through her hair. Anna closed her eyes, luxuriating in the sensation – her favourite of the day. The gentle pulling at her scalp, the soft caress of the bristles through her hair and the way Jane's hand followed the brush, petting the soft strands to smooth them. She made a small sound of pleasure, and Jane's hands stilled for a moment, then continued.

'What about you, Jane? Do you have to marry? Perhaps you have a sweetheart in the village?' When they were children they might have shared such secrets, but it had been years since they had been girls giggling together, and their stations in life had torn them apart. Anna had tutors and lessons and hunting, while Jane had been trained to service and offered a place among the staff.

'No, my Lady, there's no one. But I'm not lonely. It's a good life.'

'One you are free to choose for yourself. Sometimes I think I envy you, Jane.'

Jane smiled at her in the mirror. 'You think so, but there are freedoms and traps that each of us must deal with, and perhaps we will each always envy each other.'

'How did my maid grow so wise?' Anna teased. Truly it was wise, though that was hard to believe at a time like this, when she felt her life closing in on her. If she wanted her future son to have a title, with all of the freedoms and rights that entailed, then to give him that life she would have to give up her own freedom, at least a little, and choose a titled husband.

'I'm not wise, my Lady, just practical,' Jane said. She tied a ribbon to finish off the braid, and stepped back. The bed was already turned down, the room prepared for Anna to sleep. But although she had fully intended to do so when she'd stormed out of supper, she no longer felt tired.

'Jane, why don't you have a sweetheart?'

Jane blinked. 'There's ... no one appropriate whom I fancy, my Lady.'

'No one at all? What about inappropriate?'

'I shouldn't say, my Lady.'

And it would be wrong of Anna to use her position to push. She knew it. But she stepped towards her maid anyway, and lowered her voice. 'Come, Jane, we were girls together. If you can tell no one else, surely you can at least tell me. You must know I would never betray your confidence in me.'

Jane didn't answer with words. Instead she leaned forward and closed the small distance left between them, pressing her lips to Anna's in a charged kiss. Anna felt her head swim and her heart burst with excitement and joy at such a simple touch. It was everything she had never dared to imagine, and she revelled in it, wishing she could lose herself for ever in that simple, chaste embrace.

But Jane pulled back, looking shocked at herself, and started to turn away. Anna grabbed her arms and held her still, and the maid stared, stricken, into the middle distance. 'My Lady, forgive me.'

'Never.' Anna kissed her back, feeling her beloved Jane slowly melt from panicked stiffness into soft acceptance beneath her hands. Jane's tongue teased over her lips, and Anna whimpered and opened instinctively to welcome her in. God, the world was spinning apart and being remade anew around them, and nothing would ever look the same again.

When they fell apart this time, both of them were breathing heavily, and Jane did not try to flee, though she still looked stricken. 'It's folly, my Lady. Foolishness. I am the daughter of a cook, and you are the daughter of an earl. There is no future here. *None!*' Her eyes shone wetly, and her voice was thick.

'Don't you dare leave me over this. Promise me you won't.'

'No, my Lady. I could never leave you. Not unless you sent me away.'

'Don't be daft. How could I ever send you away when you've changed my life and opened my heart? And anyway, if you took off that maid's livery and I took off my gown, we'd be just the same.'

Jane's eyes went round with shock. 'My Lady, you mustn't do that!'

'Perhaps. But I still want to. Will you hold me?'

Jane stepped into her arms, and Anna sighed in silent pleasure as the two women held one other. She wanted Jane – wanted her in ways she should probably never even consider – but there was time yet. She stepped back and gave her maid a sad smile. 'Get on with you, and enjoy your supper. I hope it's still hot.'

'I'm sure it's been kept warm for me,' Jane said, curt-seying. Anna wished she wouldn't – not after what they'd shared, and what she still hoped to share. 'Good night, my Lady.'

'Goodnight, Jane,' Anna murmured, watching the door close behind her. She climbed into bed and pressed her eyes shut, her mind whirling with imagined images of Jane's soft skin and sweet, rounded breasts and the cries she might make in the dark of night when Anna brought her to the heights of passion. Anna slid one hand beneath her gown, and brought herself to torturous, silent pleasure.

* * *

Anna smiled politely as Lord Robert was presented to her. He was a marquess's heir, so marriage to him would technically be a step up for her, though she knew that her dowry would be important to maintaining his family's status. She dipped her head, mustering every ounce of manners she had been taught, and allowed him to lead her to a settee for quiet conversation. She was sure she was going to choke on the frustration of it all. Lord Robert was her fourth suitor, out of the six her father had apparently lined up for her inspection.

She wondered which one her father would choose, and decided it would probably be Charlie, just to vex her. He was family, after all, and it would mean that the old Earl would see his title passed on to his daughter and grand-children, but she would rather be cast into poverty than marry her idiot cousin. No, she would have to choose, so it wouldn't do to alienate any man until she'd decided.

They were to play a game of croquet in the afternoon,

with Frances and her husband, Lord Jack. Anna wasn't sure if she was looking forward to it or dreading it, but she carried herself with decorum and displayed the correct level of eagerness. Her father should be pleased, at least. He was surely expecting her to do something drastic at any moment, but she'd behave. She had to.

Behind closed doors, however, was another matter. She'd refused to let the feelings between her and Jane rest, and their kissing and caressing, especially during the times when Jane was required to dress and undress her, were growing ever more heated as the two women explored and their desire grew.

Even now, half-listening to Lord Robert chatter on about something in London, she grew flushed thinking of how, just this morning, she'd dared to slip the small red berry of Jane's nipple between her lips, licking and sucking at it to elicit delightful gasps of pleasure and arousal from her beloved maid. Jane had returned the gesture, lifting one of Anna's full breasts to her mouth and kissing it with such worshipful adoration that Anna had wondered if she could achieve the summit of pleasure from Jane's mouth alone.

Her father would probably die of shock if he ever found out, but their interludes had become as vital to Anna as air, and she thought she would die or let her father cast her out before she gave Jane up.

The day, as days with suitors went, was an easy one.

Richard was polite and kind, and though no one could hold a candle to Jane in Anna's heart, he was quite tolerable. Still, to have to marry him – to have to go to bed with him as his wife, whenever he desired it – was difficult to contemplate without feeling that familiar stirring of panic and dread.

At least, she thought so – until she entered the library one evening and found Richard speaking quietly to a footman. Before Jane, she would never have known what to look for, but with her newly experienced eye she was sure she saw the marks of forbidden desire on his face, particularly when the footman turned to leave and Richard followed the man with his eyes.

'Lord Richard,' she said, announcing herself. He spun, fixed a polite smile on his face and bowed over her hand as she offered it.

'Just the lady my eyes were desperate to see,' he said.

'I don't think it's a lady you're desperate for at all.' It was a gamble to say it. He was the best of the lot, and, if he were insulted, she would have driven off her most promising suitor, but ... her eyes flicked toward the door through which the footman had left, and Richard paled slightly before recovering.

'Why, of course I do! Especially one of such breeding and beauty as yourself, my lovely Anna.'

'Indeed. I fancy a walk in the garden. Will you join me?'

115

He glanced toward the windows, which were dark with night. 'Is that appropriate, Lady Anna?'

She smiled. 'I doubt it, but I think we should talk. Lord Richard, I think we have more to gain from an alliance than even you realise.'

He was intrigued, she could tell. And puzzled. He glanced around as if expecting the censorious arrival of her father at any moment, but, when he didn't immediately burst in upon them, Richard offered her his arm.

She led him to the darkest part of the garden, well away from the main house and any prying eyes or listening ears. 'I am in love, Lord Richard,' she said. It was the most dangerous way to start this conversation, but she knew in her heart that she was right. And if she was, it would probably be the most effective. She prayed she was not about to ruin herself, but the thought of Jane made her bold enough to risk it.

'What? With me, Lady?' He stopped, shocked, and turned to her.

'With my maid. Jane. And I think that perhaps you would be sympathetic to someone in such a plight.'

He stared at her for long moments, a thousand thoughts flashing behind his eyes as he took in the implications of this conversation. 'You propose an alliance of convenience. But Anna, my family must have an heir, whatever my personal desires.'

'Yes. I'm a well-born lady, and, whoever I marry, an

heir will be the price of my position. I accept that.' She put a hand on his chest, leaning close, seducing him not with her body, but with everything else she could offer. 'We will lie together to produce our heir, my Lord. And I shall lie with no other*man*, and you with no other *woman*, just as a husband and wife should.'

'My dear lady, I'm quite sure I don't deserve you,' he said, his voice still thoughtful. She held her breath and watched his eyes, thoughtful under the light of the moon.

'I hope … I hope that you will have me anyway.'

'Marriage to you would solve many of my problems, Lady Anna. How could I do any less than to solve some of yours?' He took her hand, squeezing it in imitation of a handshake, and kissed her knuckles. 'Shall I tell your father that we are announcing our engagement?'

That night, Anna felt as if she could have danced her way up the stairs to bed. Her parents thought she had fallen in love with Lord Richard. Let them. The secret smiles they exchanged were not those of two people who adored each other, however, but those of two who shared a delightful secret.

Anna rang for Jane, who appeared only moments later, looking worried. 'I heard you accepted a suit, my Lady!'

'I did indeed,' and she twirled with excitement. 'Oh, Jane, I can't wait to tell you! He's perfect!'

Jane's face became a neutral mask, and her skin turned

117

to the colour of fresh ash. 'I see. Good news, my Lady. I'm happy for you.'

'Oh, Jane, don't think I'm putting you aside. Don't think it for a second!' She grabbed her maid and pulled the woman close, pressing their bodies together with desperate fondness. 'I don't love him, you silly girl, I love you. It will always be you.'

'But Lord Richard ...'

'The marquis and I apparently share a certain perversion,' Anna said, her voice wry. 'We must produce an heir – that we can't escape – but he shall be free to give his heart to the man he chooses, just as I am free to give mine to you.'

Jane froze as the words registered. She opened her mouth, shut it and opened it again without making a sound.

'Say something, won't you? You will come with me, Jane? Say you'll come with me to my new household and be mine.'

'Yours?' Jane squeaked.

'Mine. My heart. And I shall be yours. Please, say you'll come.'

'Mine? My Lady ... *my* Lady?'

'Say my name.'

'Anna,' Jane breathed. 'My Anna. Of course.'

Anna nearly sobbed with relief as she swept the other woman into her arms. She kissed her deeply, letting her tongue tease across Jane's lips with the expertise she'd gained over their months of secretive practice. Soon she'd be wed, and have her own room in her own household, where Jane would be allowed to share her space and her life, at least privately. Heaven!

The joy of it came tumbling out of her, spilling from her heart and infecting Jane until their passions had them both reaching for buttons and ties, fumbling in their haste, laughing and kissing whatever they could reach.

When Jane stood entirely naked before her for the first time, Anna saw that she'd been right. 'You see?' she whispered 'We're just the same.' They kissed again, a deep, sweet kiss that swept both of them away. Then Anna took Jane's hand and led her to the large turned-down bed. She longed to give Jane the same sweet pleasure she'd given herself night after night with Jane's scent still in her mind.

She dipped her fingers into Jane's folds, finding them as hot and slick as she'd ever found her own, and teased at the opening at the centre before sliding her finger up to find that hard nub of pleasure she'd so often caressed on her own body. Jane gasped and sighed, struggling with the urge to cry out, and Anna paused, smiling as she waited for her lover to catch her breath. She lifted her fingers to her own lips and licked away the sweet cream that had collected there.

Then she returned to her sensual attack, rubbing and

119

teasing as she had done so often to herself until Jane buried her face in Anna's neck and cried out with pleasure. Nearly sobbing, Jane pushed Anna back until she lay atop her, their naked bodies soft and yielding as they pressed together and their legs tangled.

'Is this a dream?' Jane asked. 'Is my heart killing me with a foolish dream of my most secret desires?'

'Not unless I'm dreaming, too. Soon, my love, my Jane, soon we will share a bed and a life, for real. For ever.'

'For ever,' Jane whispered. She moved to kiss Anna, and Anna cried out softly as the other woman shifted and sent a bolt of pleasure from between her legs. Jane saw and smiled softly, shifting her hips again in the same way, building up a rhythm that soon had Anna stifling her cries with her own hand and rising beneath her.

When the pleasure washed through her, she threw her head back and whimpered, amazed at how much ecstasy one body could contain. Jane laughed quietly and kissed Anna until she was breathing normally again.

'I need to get back downstairs before I'm missed,' Jane said, sounding reluctant. 'Shall I braid your hair?'

'We've taken too long, I can manage. But Jane?' Her maid paused, half-dressed. 'When we have our own bed together, I shall delight in making you scream my name.' Jane's face was still flushed and smiling when she finished dressing and hurried out of the room.

The Architect
Mina Murray

Lady Hargreave had sent her man to meet me at the station and I was grateful for the escort, for it was bitterly cold out and growing bleaker by the minute. Once Ralph handed my bags into the carriage and joined the driver in the front, I was much more comfortable and free to ruminate at my leisure while watching the countryside, such as I could see of it, roll by.

When the summons had arrived from Hartfield, I had meant to attend to it immediately, but the death of my father intervened. The business of settling his affairs drew me north and detained me longer than anticipated. The Hargreaves had originally expected me in May, when spring would show the house and its grounds to best advantage, but it was now November and I was uncertain of my welcome. Nonetheless, it was a great relief to leave the London smog behind. I could feel my head and

121

my lungs clearing as we travelled deeper into the woods surrounding the estate. I must have dozed, for the next thing I knew we had slowed down and a pair of heavy iron gates swung open to admit us.

I'll never forget my first sight of that place, its battlements rising shadowed out of the gloaming, its spires and finials threatening to pierce the clouds that hung darkly overhead as the last remnants of daylight faded away.

A lone figure stood at the end of the drive to greet me.

'Wentworth?'

'The same, sir.'

The butler had a dour look about him. Whether that was his customary appearance or an attempt at gravitas I don't know. He eyed me warily.

'If you'll allow me to take your coat, I'll show you to the library. Lady Hargreave will be with you presently.'

She was not. She kept me waiting for the better part of an hour. I occupied myself by perusing Rufus Hargreave's superbly appointed library, which boasted several volumes so rare I was almost loath to touch them.

As the minutes dragged by, I found myself growing irritable. I was tired, hungry and, I admit, insulted. While the Hargreaves were paying for my services, I was a gentleman of some renown in my own right and they knew very well I was not relying on their fee to keep myself. I had not been forced into taking up an occupation. I had *elected* to do so, rather than idling my life away in drawing rooms or gentlemen's clubs or, worse, pontificating in the House of Lords. By the time the library door opened again I had worked myself into a righteous state.

The woman who entered was not at all what I expected. She was attired simply, in a plain green dress without a bustle or the puffed sleeves that were currently in fashion but forced the wearer to negotiate doorways at a forty-five-degree angle. Her quick step and bright eyes spoke of action, intelligence and wit and none of the indolence so typical of the highborn ladies I usually met.

'You must be the architect. We were beginning to despair of your ever arriving.'

'Charles Morgan, my Lady, at your service.'

She laughed.

'I am no Lady, sir. I am Felicity Drummond, Lady Hargreave's companion. She is indisposed, and asked me to welcome you on her behalf.'

Ah.

'Now, Mr Morgan, we do usually dress for dinner, but we shan't stand on ceremony tonight. No doubt you have a prodigious appetite after your long journey.'

I could not have wished for better company. Miss Drummond's conversation was intelligent and well informed; neither too serious nor too frivolous. Never before had I been so immediately at ease with a woman. The prospect of spending several weeks in residence at

123

Hartfield – undoing the architectural outrages it had suffered at the hands of its former master, a man with more money than taste – seemed rather a joy than a labour.

* * *

It was several days before I met Lady Hargreave, whose continuing ill health kept her confined above stairs. I had been on my way to join Ralph for a tour of the grounds when Wentworth appeared and conducted me to her sitting room. Lady Hargreave was settled on a divan, a book open on her lap.

'Please, do sit down.' She motioned to the armchair beside her. 'Mountebank, wasn't it?'

'Morgan, your Ladyship.'

'Oh, yes, of course. My husband was impressed with the work you accomplished on the Templetons' estate.'

'Is he expected back soon?'

'Not for a month, at least. Rufus is on the Continent, attaché to a diplomatic mission. I should like your sketches to be complete before he returns.'

'Did he leave any particular instructions?'

'None, other than to correct the house's anomalies of style. You may refer any questions to Felicity. She is authorised to speak for me, and has an excellent knowledge of the house.'

Throughout the tête-à-tête that followed, I got the

sense that she was taking my measure, for some obscure reason. The directness of her gaze was most unnerving.

She stood to indicate that our interview was over. The hand she extended was slender and elegant and tipped with severely filed nails that looked capable of drawing blood. Her grip was surprisingly firm for one reputed to be ill. But then illness came in many forms, not all of them physically manifest.

Over the few weeks, I saw little of Lady Hargreave but a great deal of Miss Drummond. She soon became an asset to my work, demonstrating a particular facility for draughtsmanship. We spent many a rainy afternoon closeted in the library, sketching the proposed modifications. It was on one such afternoon that I realised I was in love with her.

Felicity was seated by the window, writing in her journal, and I had been staring at her for a full quarter of an hour. Her mouth especially fascinated me. It was full and generous and ruby red, and she bit it enticingly when absorbed in thought, as she was now. I ducked my head, hoping she hadn't noticed. While we had a genuine rapport and she seemed to enjoy my company, that did not necessarily translate into a deeper regard. I had no desire to make a fool of myself by declaring my affections without being more certain of hers.

I received a sign sooner than I'd hoped. We were walking in the greenhouse the very next day when I said something amusing that made her laugh, and she threw her arms about my neck and kissed me. So great was my surprise that I did not immediately reciprocate. She must have misinterpreted this as a lack of interest, or, worse, as offence, for she pulled back immediately.

'Oh, Charles,' she cried, 'oh, Mr Morgan, forgive me!'

Her expression was stricken; her eyes brimmed with unshed tears.

'Please, you must say something!'

'"The curves of your lips rewrite history."'

'Charles, do not mock me!' She stamped her foot, and I was heartened by her anger, which was infinitely preferable to despair. 'This is serious.'

'So am I,' I replied, and bent to kiss her.

Everything about her was like a drug to me, some powerful opiate that clouded my judgement and blinded me to propriety. She smelled like lavender, and her soft lips tasted of honey as I coaxed them open. She seemed to know what to do instinctively, for her tongue began to play with mine and she rubbed herself against me, gripping the lapels of my coat to keep me close.

Without breaking the kiss, I walked us some ways forward, until her back was against the greenhouse wall. My cock was as stiff as a fencepost and I'm ashamed to say that I pressed my hardness against her softness and plundered her mouth with rather more intensity than I had intended.

The sound of footsteps outside, the crunch of gravel, brought me to my senses and I released her. Her shoulders slumped against the wall, palms pressed flat against it for support. A moment later John walked past the window; I don't believe he saw us. I was grateful to him for the interruption, though. Another minute and I would have plunged one hand under Felicity's skirts and the other under my breeches and manipulated us both to climax.

When I was sure the danger of discovery had passed, I reached out to cup her chin in my hands.

'Look at me, love, there's no need for shame.'

'No shame, Charles,' she said softly, raising her eyes to mine. 'Merely modesty.'

A lock of hair had come loose from her coiffure. I twirled the silken strands between my fingers.

She seemed surprised at the tenderness, and a shadow crossed her face. When I asked what troubled her, she merely shook her head. So I kissed the tip of her nose; and she smiled at me; and all was right again. We walked back to the house slowly, careful to stay a respectable distance apart.

* * *

The days that followed were the closest I'd ever come to perfect happiness. My work at Hartfield – and certain other preparations I was making – was almost complete

127

when Felicity approached me with a sparkle in her eyes and a sheaf of yellowed papers in her hand.

'Charles, look – I found the original plans of the house!'

She spread out one of the fragile sheets, and pointed to a cross-hatched area along the right-hand side of the house.

'It's a secret passageway! We must explore it at once.'

Felicity grabbed my hand and pulled me along behind her. Sure enough, carved into the wall, easily missed unless one was looking for it, was the symbol of a torch. We pushed it together, it depressed, and a panel of the wall sprang open. After lighting the candle she had brought, we groped our way down the dark passage. Our footfalls were muted by the long carpet runner that lined the narrow corridor, and just as well, for shortly we heard voices clear as day from the other side.

'Listen,' whispered Felicity, 'that's Cook's voice. We must be right near the kitchens.'

I stumbled in the near-darkness and banged my elbow on something. My groan must have carried further than I thought.

'Angels and ministers of grace defend us,' shrieked Cook, as she dropped what sounded like the soup cauldron. 'I knew this place was haunted!'

Felicity shook with mirth, the candle waving so precariously I feared she'd set the place ablaze. I took the waxy pillar from her and set it in a wall sconce, and she came to me as I'd hoped she would, unpinning her hair and letting it cascade in golden waves around her shoulders.

The knowledge that we were well and truly alone seemed to free something in her, for she embraced me without her customary shyness and pressed teasing little kisses to my mouth, and down my neck, and finally all over my chest, unbuttoning my shirt as she went. I shrugged out of the garment as soon as I could and was soon divested of my undershirt.

Felicity began to smooth her hands over my muscles in slow, hypnotic strokes. My eyes closed in pleasure, and I imagined myself lying naked in my bed, with Felicity's small hands curling around my prick, struggling to encompass my rapidly increasing girth.

She stopped to gaze up at me with those big eyes of hers, filled with a need she would not name.

'Charles,' she whispered, 'there are ... that is, I have heard ...'

'What is it, love? Tell me.'

'There are things a man and a woman may do, Charles,' she burst out, 'that will bring them great pleasure, without risk of a child.'

That Liss would know this, desired to *do* this, set my blood on fire.

'Yes, my clever girl, yes, there are. And I would like to try all of them with you.'

She hid her face against my chest, but that suited me

well. It meant that I could clasp her to me, pull us both down to the ground, and settle her body over mine until we were pressed together from tip to toe.

'Kiss me,' I murmured, 'kiss me and I will show you.'

Liss went wild for me then, squirming atop me til I could hardly bear it. Her hands slipped between our bodies to wrestle with my breeches; eagerness made her clumsy. After what felt like an eternity of the most agonising anticipation, she finally succeeded, but by then the gesture was almost redundant. With each button she'd undone, her hands had caressed me. In the end my prick was so painfully hard I'm sure it could have burst free without any assistance at all. I did lift my hips, though, so she could tug my breeches down about my ankles.

She settled back on her heels, and for a moment she was still. Her eyes traversed the length of my body, my thighs, the sickle-shaped scar beneath my ribcage, the scattering of dark hair over my chest. I felt at once how exciting it was to be bare when she was fully clothed, to have her sit there and just look at me so brazenly, to study the curve of my cock and the way my foreskin had drawn back so she could see the swollen tip in all its russet-shining glory. Could she really think me – *it* – beautiful? It certainly seemed so, for she was biting her lip and her cheeks had pinkened and she reached for me as if under a compulsion.

'May I?'

'I wish you would!' I groaned, voice hoarse with need.

Is there anything more sublime in all the world than the feeling of skin on skin? At first Liss handled me tentatively, as if she were afraid she'd hurt me. But just when I was about to tell her she needn't worry, that I enjoyed a firm hand, she set to tugging at me in a rough rhythm that made my toes curl. She watched my every move, the way my breath came heavier when her thumb rubbed my frenulum, the way I jumped when she hit some other particularly delicious spot.

With every new discovery she made, she grew bolder and her technique more assured. Soon she was working me with one hand while the other moved to circle my balls. I tried to thrust up into her hand, but she drew back, and I gnashed my teeth in frustration at the pleasure withheld so cruelly.

'Be patient, Charles,' she entreated, 'there is one more thing I should like to do.'

My heart skipped a beat as she bent forward and licked me with long, wide sweeps of her tongue, and I arched my back for her like a woman. After she had tasted me so, she trapped my straining shaft between her two hands, dragging them slowly upwards and taking my very soul with her.

'"Palm to palm" –' I gasped, as her steepled fingers enclosed my cockhead like a cage.

'– "is holy palmer's kiss"? Are you speaking in verse from now on?' she teased. 'Sir, this is too much.'

'Then stop my mouth with a kiss.'

She leaned forward, and I took great pleasure in redirecting her.

'No, Liss –' my voice was sly '– a kiss from your *other* lips. Slip out of your drawers and kneel over me, and we'll both take our pleasure at the same time.'

The look of shock on her face was gratifying; even more so because she proceeded to do just as I'd asked. Then her voluminous skirts covered my head like a hood, and everything went dark, and I felt my way to her like a blind man.

The moment I tasted her I knew I would never let her go. I kissed her gently at first, mindful that she was new to this, but then excitement got the better of me and I tongued her passionately, tracing the silken folds of her cunt as if I were an explorer mapping some undiscovered continent.

With a cry, she fell forward and took me into the hot wet cavern of her mouth. I was no green lad – I had bedded my share of women on several continents – but no one in the world could touch my Liss. Her wicked pink tongue teased me in ways I had never dreamed of, and never wanted to end.

I thrust my hand under her bodice and grabbed hold of the laces of her corset, winding them tight around my palm to make sure she couldn't move. The extra constriction seemed to please her, for her movements suddenly grew frantic, and I flicked insistently at her bud with the tip of my tongue and let her grind her cunny against my face.

We took our fill of each other thus, with half of the household bustling on the other side of the wall. Felicity sobbed as she came, and it made my heart swell with manly pride to know that I had pleased her, and that she had swallowed my seed.

Afterward, she nestled at my side, resting her hand on my heart.

'Felicity – *Liss* –' I had been rehearsing this speech for almost a week, but found now that I could remember nothing save the unadorned sentiments of my heart.

'I love you, Liss. Make me happy for ever, and marry me?'

In the silence that followed, I thought – as I had so many times before – of the shadow that had crossed her face that day in the greenhouse.

She pressed a kiss to my ear, then whispered: 'Yes. Yes, Charles, I will marry you. Yes.'

I knew words would be insufficient to express my joy, so I did the only thing that would, and buried my head under her skirts again.

* * *

I should have slept serenely that night, having secured Felicity's hand. Instead, though, my sleep was restless. I woke from a nightmare and, too shaken to return to bed, began to walk the halls.

I don't know what force persuaded me to enter the wing of the house where Lady Hargreave's rooms were, but I did. Perhaps the house itself was directing me, anxious to share its knowledge, to finally yield up its secrets in mute surrender. As I trailed my hand along the wall, I discovered another symbol, identical to the one marking the hidden passage downstairs. When I pressed it, a door swung smoothly open.

I followed the passageway for some time, until I heard Felicity's familiar voice. To my right, carved into the wall at eye level, were two holes. I had seen these before, in another old house. There would be a portrait on the other side of the wall, with eyes that followed you wherever you went.

I fought with my conscience but, when I heard Lady Hargreave's voice as well, the battle was over. The two women were in their nightgowns, Lady Hargreave sitting in bed propped up with pillows, and Felicity standing at the foot of the bed, slightly to one side. They were arguing.

'This is the last time, Vivian. I love Charles, and I will marry him, within the week.'

'I forbid it!'

'It's not your decision. I've loved you dearly, you know that, but you must let me go now.'

Lady Hargreave was weeping. There was a regal grandeur to her tear-stained face.

'We have tonight. Let that be enough,' Felicity beseeched, 'and please don't cry.'

With that she reached up and plucked at the ribbons tied at each shoulder, and her gown fluttered to the ground. She stood there for a moment, displaying a body just as lush as I had imagined, before climbing onto the bed and stripping her mistress naked as well. The two women embraced then, their bodies a study in contrasts, Felicity golden-haired, rosy and voluptuous, and Vivian dark-haired, pale and lithe. I knew I should have looked away, if only to spare myself, but found that I could not. Jealousy and anger roiled in my gut, but these enflamed, rather than dampened, my arousal. I released my cock-stand and stroked myself as I watched the women pleasure each other with lips and fingers, teeth and tongues.

When Vivian produced an ivory phallus and made her lover take it into her mouth, I wondered for a moment whether she intended to assert *ius primae noctis* and take Felicity's virginity for herself. The thought stirred such dark fantasies inside me that I half-wished she would do it. I would be powerless to stop it, could do nothing but watch, sick with lust and despair, as Felicity, the little traitor, raised her hips to welcome that piercing thrust. Vivian would pull out the phallus then and rub it over her breasts, adorning herself like some pagan goddess after the hunt. She would be magnificent, and terrible, and I would understand why she was worthy of Felicity's worship.

But I would still want to revenge the theft of her maidenhood. I would burst into the room, and snatch up the jar of night cream on the dressing table and then throw Vivian face down on the bed. I'd ruck up her nightgown, and spread the cream over the winking star of her arse. She'd make a half-hearted protest when I readied her with my fingers, but then, when I finally drove my prick into her, she'd make a guttural sound that I would never have heard from a woman before and thrust back, enveloping me in her tightness and heat.

The cries from the other room grew louder, and I saw Felicity riding Vivian's leg as she fucked her mistress with that ivory phallus.

When Felicity reached her peak, Vivian looked toward my hiding place with an exultant glare in her cat-green eyes. She held my gaze, never wavering, as her own body was racked with pleasure. That Vivian had likely known I was watching them the whole time affected me intensely, and I came so violently it hurt. My seed spurted out in a great arc, spattering the panel in front of me, then slipping down it in an opalescent trail.

Before I could recover, there were footsteps, and then the scraping sound of a sliding door, and I barely had time to pull up my trousers before I tumbled into the room at Vivian's feet. She towered over me, naked and imperious.

'Did you think, Mr Morgan, that I do not know every inch of this house, including all its secret egresses?'

She reached out a hand to help me up. My voice was steadier than my legs.

'No, Lady Hargreave.'

I bowed.

She laughed then, a short bark, more rueful than amused.

'Well, Felicity, at least his manners are sound, for all he is a Peeping Tom.'

My fiancée had the grace to look embarrassed.

'I'll leave you two alone for now,' Vivian said. 'Please refrain from fornicating in my bed.'

I hardly knew how to react in such a situation, but my body decided for me and I walked over to where Felicity lay, tangled in her mistress's twisted sheets.

'We have some matters to say to each other, Felicity, which will keep until the morning. But this you must know – my feelings for you are unchanged.'

As proof, I bent down to kiss the points of her exquisite breasts.

'I love you,' she moaned, and wound her arms around

my neck and pulled me down beside her. I meant to protest, but then her hand curled around me and, well, how could I deny her?

When Lady Hargreave returned, she did not seem perturbed. Her colour was high, and there was a gleam in her eyes that I recognised.

'Since you are still here, and technically in my employ until tomorrow, Mr Morgan,' she said, spreading her legs, 'there is one more thing that I want done, and you look like just the man.'

Peekaboo Lace
Flora Dain

The lace peignoir flowed down her body with a sensuous whisper. As it swirled around her feet Lucilla sighed with pleasure. When had she last worn something like this?

The hour was late, but in the grand reception rooms downstairs a ball was in full swing. Music and chatter echoed all through the great house, all the way up to her tiny room.

Sadly she was not invited. She was not even a guest.

She was working here, doing a favour to a friend. By day she went by an assumed name, scraped back her hair and quietly performed her tasks.

Only by night could she be herself.

Leaving off her finery was a poor disguise but here she was unlikely to run into anyone she knew.

Sometimes friends came at a high price.

Creeping downstairs in search of a drink of water she'd

spotted the lace laid out in one of the master bedrooms, the filmy silk a heap of dark roses scattered over the bed. *Black lace?* How intriguing.

It had taken only a second to dart in for a closer look. She ran it though her fingers, entranced, and then buried her face in its gossamer softness.

How would it feel to *wear?*

Whisking it back to her room she had stepped quickly out of her modest gown and stays, held it aloft and slipped it over her head. In the faint light of her one candle her skin glowed through the pattern of finely wrought flowers. They skimmed and clung in surprising places, swelling her curves, pinching her waist, swirling free of her long legs with provocative abandon.

It felt wonderful, but what must it *look* like?

She had to see it.

The tiny mirror in her room showed hardly anything but down near the main staircase there was a huge looking glass placed directly under the great chandelier over the stairwell. There she would get a full view … and everyone was dancing. No one would see.

She ran lightly on bare feet down the rough wooden staircase to the wider corridor of the imposing second floor. Her toes sank into thick carpet, a reminder of more missed luxury.

Seconds later she caught sight of herself. From the huge mirror an enchantress from ancient legend gazed

140

back at her, naked under the lace, her dark eyes luminous with excitement.

Lucilla held her breath. In the hot beam of nearly fifty candles she looked back at her reflection in triumphant shock and then pirouetted happily.

Her naked skin gleamed like pearl under the dark film of lace, her narrow waist, long legs and swelling breasts clearly visible. Her nipples glowed a deep, rosy red through gaps in the flowers. The dark patch at the apex of her thighs was a tempting, murky shadow.

The next instant she felt a shift in the air, coolness on her skin. A ripple of fear ran through her. *Supposing someone should see?*

'Exquisite.' A rich male voice echoed around her.

She spun round and clapped a hand to her mouth as a man emerged from the shadows.

He swept her with a look of intense satisfaction. 'I pray to the heavens for something – *anything* – to liven up this ghastly ball and they send me a gift, an Angel of the Night.' He moved up close. 'I should pray more often.'

She gazed up at him, torn between the urge to flee and an overwhelming desire to stay. He was startlingly handsome, with strong features, a sculpted mouth and an intelligent gaze. He moved with the easy grace of the predator and the very rich.

Her mind raced. This must be the star guest, the prize

the lady of the house had hoped to lure for her daughter with this evening's ball.

Lucilla swallowed. 'You are not dancing, sir?'

He eyed her calmly. 'I'd sooner watch you. Please, oblige me by turning again.'

Now. Lucilla made a dash for the stairs but he was too quick for her.

In a single bound he caught her by the waist in a powerful grip. 'Not so fast, my Lady. In here, quickly, before we're seen.'

Her blood ran cold. To be caught like this would be a terrible scandal.

Play along for now – slip away later.

He pushed her through a doorway and slammed it behind them with the heel of his boot. She looked around her in amazement. Compared to her tiny room his suite was magnificent. The high ceilings were elaborately painted, the walls lined with damask. Through an open doorway she glimpsed a large bed, and beyond it tall windows draped with silk and open to the soft night air.

He had still not relaxed his hold. 'So, Madame, what brings you to my door?'

'Forgive me, sir, I thought everyone was downstairs. I simply wanted to –'

He folded both his arms round her waist, leant down and fastened his lips on her neck. She stood very still, her heart racing as flames sprang from his touch, sending shivers all over her skin.

His hair was faintly scented. Some light, elusive blend of citrus was mingled with something else, something *male*. It acted on her senses like wine.

'Simply wanted to – what? Torment me?' Slowly he turned her round to face him and he descended again, this time fastening his mouth on her throat. She felt helpless in his arms, overcome with a wave of longing so acute she felt a throb deep between her legs.

How did he do this? She leaned back, arching her neck with a contented sigh. His hands explored her body, gentle but relentless as he traced the curve of her hips, the narrow inlet of her waist, the swell of her breasts.

'Deuce, Madame, the sight of you thrills the soul. I had begun to despair of this evening. Come, some champagne. Then you can dance for me some more.'

* * *

On a small gilded table an open bottle of champagne was waiting, cradled in a bucket of ice. He poured two glasses and passed one to her, eyeing her over the rim as they sipped. 'So why do you parade at my door in peekaboo lace?'

She eyed him from under her lashes. *Two could play*

143

at this. 'How else would an Angel of the Night lure her prey, sir?'

What had she said?

His smile vanished. Quietly he set both their glasses down on the table and pulled her into his arms. His mouth descended on hers with a finality that robbed her of breath, his tongue surging along her own in an invasion of heat and spice that dissolved her will.

It had been so long ...

She responded eagerly, pressing herself against him, winding her fingers up into his short hair, revelling in the feel of his jutting erection hard against her belly. He explored her, his hands moulding and teasing her breasts, sliding between her thighs. Flames spurted into life everywhere he touched, making her skin a riot of fire and sparks.

As he pulled away he gazed down at her with an expression so intense she felt her legs weaken.

'Deuce, Madame, your powers are too dark for an angel. A devil, rather.'

He pushed her hard against the wall, his mouth descending on her throat, his lips hot and fierce as he dropped kisses down its length to the swell of her breasts, and then took a mouthful of breast and lace and sucked hard.

She cried out at the pleasure of it as he teased her nipple first with his tongue and then with his teeth, one hand pinning her to the wall by her wrists, the other searching deep between her thighs, cupping her with strong, warm fingers, pressing, squeezing, sending waves of heat coursing through her.

He released her and fastened on the other breast, his laughter muffled as she cried out again in mock protest.

'Hold still, Madame. Do you want the whole house to hear? It's lucky my valet's below stairs chasing maids or we'd have an audience.'

'Truly, sir, you are mistaken. I'd no idea you were here. And you should ask permission.'

Startled, he jerked up his head, eyes blazing. 'What's this? You'd display your full glory in black lace and then *deny* me? You were hoping to meet someone else?'

Her eyes widened. 'No, sir, truly. I wanted only to see the effect. I thought everyone was in the ballroom.'

His slow smile masked a meaningful gleam. 'And now you have seen the effect are you satisfied?'

She arched her neck as a fresh wave of desire coursed through her. '*Satisfied*, sir? Hardly. But we make a promising start.' She smiled at him serenely.

His jaw tensed. Holding her gaze he gently dipped his finger in the wine and held it over her face. 'And you came here for what? Another taste, Angel?'

She eyed him steadily, sensing his power, and then slowly extended her tongue and licked the end of his finger.

His dark eyes narrowed. 'Ah. I see we understand one another.'

He trailed his other hand gently down her throat and along the curve of her breast. She held her breath, expecting a kiss, but instead he swept her up in his arms, carried her to the bed and dropped her onto the heavy silk cover.

He seized the soft cord holding back the drapes at the bed head and wrenched it off the fitting. In seconds he had tied her wrists to the posts, stretching her arms across the soft pillows and fastening each side securely.

She stared up at him in shock. 'What are you going to do?'

'You'll see.'

His smile had faded. It was replaced with a look of intense concentration. She gasped as he hauled at her feet, splayed them wide and tugged at the other cord. It came away in his hands with a snap, the heavy gold tassels brushing her navel as he tested its length and wound it round first one ankle and then the other until she was securely spread-eagled across the quilt.

'Now, Madame, we shall have you satisfied.'

She watched mesmerised as he unfastened his shirt and tugged it over his head, loosened his trousers and kicked off his boots. As his body emerged from the snowy linen, bronzed and gleaming, she bit her lip and then tugged at her bonds in an automatic move to lean across and touch him.

He leaned over her as his erection sprang free and she gasped as its hard, silky heat brushed against her belly.

'You struggle so soon? We've hardly started.'

With infinite patience he leaned down and touched his lips to her navel, teasing her with the tip of his tongue. She stilled as he dropped kisses all across her belly, and then moved down her left thigh and laid another trail of soft, delicate kisses along the inside curve, kneeling over her with his legs either side of her shoulders.

She gazed at his erection looming above her, impossibly large. She could feel the heat from it on her face. He worked his way upwards with his tongue and his lips, following with long sweeps of his fingers, inflaming her, soothing her, then teasing her again until she writhed with distress.

All the while his erection loomed above her, a cruel reminder that pleasure was still out of reach, beyond her touch or taste but biding its time until he should unleash it. Soon he had reached her core, and she cried out as his mouth fastened greedily at the apex of her thighs and his tongue found her sweetest spot and pressed home.

As her pleasure began to build she pleaded for release but he silenced her by leaning up and transferring his kiss to her lips.

'Hush, be patient, or you will peak too soon. We have a whole night ahead of us. You come when I say so.'

He kneeled up over her and held his shaft high over her face, smiling as she extended her tongue to lick the base.

Its taste was exciting, salty and rough. She teased him with the tip of her tongue, daring him to give her more.

He watched her with a calm smile, his arrogance sparking her arousal, and then shifted a little so she could just reach the head. 'You would satisfy me too? Your blessings overpower me, Angel.'

Quietly he directed her to please him, leaning back to massage and fondle her throbbing centre, laughing as she writhed, soothing when she groaned. As he teased and probed her with his fingers she strained against him, aching for release, but he pulled away at the last moment and loomed once more over her face. 'Now let me see it fill your mouth.'

Denied her rapture yet again and still burning for him, her body now tense as a bowstring, she leaned up eagerly to suck him, feeling her desire mount with every lick. Slowly he eased into her, shifting so she could reach, easing back so she could savour the salty taste of his skin, letting his flavour fill her mouth and fuel her desire.

'Deuce, Madame, you're good.'

As he quivered in her mouth she sensed a change in his erection but with a groan he pulled away and stood upright. For a second she wondered if she had displeased him. He left the room for a moment and came back with the champagne.

She watched entranced at the sight of his perfect body moving across the room, lithe as a cat, rippling with finely toned muscle. He was breathtaking – very big, very erect and distinctly aroused. Her very own classical statue, but alive, prowling with lust, and intent on just one thing – *possession*.

Deep between her legs heat flared again.

She must wear lace more often.

As he drew near he took a swig from the bottle and then knelt between her legs and fastened his mouth on her sex. The tiny bubbles sparkled and fizzed on her swollen, lustful folds like a shower of sparks. His tongue followed, hot, urgent and probing. As its tip found her target her climax exploded like a volcano.

She writhed as waves of pleasure crashed over her. He held her tight while the spasms rocked through her, stifling her moans with a long, lingering kiss that swelled her pleasure with honey.

As her upheavals faded he pulled away, laughing softly, took another swig of champagne and this time kissed it gently into her mouth and then buried his face in her hair. 'Satisfied *now*, my Lady?'

She let out a contented sigh. 'Only when you are, my Lord.'

Her soft whisper seemed to surprise him. With a startled smile and a swift kiss he rapidly unfastened her limbs. 'Your concern for my pleasure earns you your freedom, my Angel. And now to the business.' He flipped her over, hauled her up by the hips, and thrust deep inside her, filling her belly with glorious heat.

His long rapid thrusts invaded her, compelling her to tense around him, her own climax building again as he braced her with one hand deep between her legs. She flexed to his stroke, hauling him deep, thrilling to the weight and heat of his body covering her back. Soon, helpless in his grasp, she came with a joyful shriek.

Her orgasm seemed to go on and on, but as her spasms clutched at him she made a conquest of her own. With a mighty shout he paused, quivered and then bucked his fluid into her until she thought she would faint from pleasure.

* * *

After the brilliance of the ball, the morning was gloomy. In the spacious entrance hall rain drummed ceaselessly on the windows, watched in silence by heavy-eyed footmen.

Few guests were about. No one paid much attention to the slim figure draped in a cloak and seated next to a small valise.

Lucilla sighed. Her stay had been cut short. She would have to make other plans.

At that moment two figures came slowly downstairs. The lady of the house was regaling a gentleman guest with the delights planned for the rest of his stay.

He was stifling a yawn.

'... And when the rain stops we shall take tea in the gardens. My daughter will dance in the summer house by the lake ...'

At the foot of the stairs he paused. 'Who is that?'

Lucilla froze as her lover from the night before swept her with a glacial stare.

His hostess looked taken aback. '*Her?* No one, your Grace. I've turned her out of the house.'

He frowned. 'She is a servant here?'

'Merely a visitor helping the lawyer with some papers. Now, here is the morning room –'

His tone became icy. 'So you turned her *out?*'

The Countess drew a sharp breath. 'Stand up, girl, when the Duke of Arven approaches you. There was a minor *fracas* this morning over a missing ... garment. It was seen in her room by one of the maids.'

Lucilla reddened. *The lace.* She'd slipped away in the early light meaning to return it but she'd fallen asleep ...

She kept her eyes resolutely ahead.

'And she is still here?'

With an effort Lady Constance reigned in her temper. 'She awaits a wagon to take her to the main road. Now, if you will step this way –'

The Duke arched an eyebrow. 'A *wagon*? Let her walk, Madame. She can reflect on her errors.'

Flustered, the Countess hailed a footman. 'Cancel the wagon.'

Lucilla gasped. 'But Lady Constance, my valise –' She broke off in dismay.

How could he? It must be a good twenty miles to the nearest coaching point.

He turned away with another yawn. 'The young woman can leave her bag here. My man will drop it at the first inn we pass for her to collect.'

The Countess looked alarmed. 'But – surely you're not *leaving*, your Grace?'

He bowed. 'Sadly, yes. I have pressing business in town. Convey my apologies to your charming daughter.'

As they moved away Lucilla ground her teeth. What had Shakespeare said?

Put not your faith in princes – or in lovers.

Especially dukes.

She snatched at her hood, gripped the cloak tightly under her chin and headed towards the main door.

* * *

An hour later she was soaked through, her boots heavy with mud. At this rate her journey would take hours. But the exercise might help her forget.

After such a night, to sink to this …

What must he think?

It was hard not to feel bitter. Did a favour to a friend have to cost so much?

From the lane behind her came the rattle of harness and the thud of pounding hooves. She shrank into the hedgerow as the great coach clattered past, splattering her with mud.

A little way ahead it slowed to a halt. Steam rose off the backs of the horses as the door swung open, bright with the colours of the Arven crest.

It must be him. She stumbled towards it, clambered up the step and sank gratefully into the soft padding of the upholstery.

The Duke was sprawled on the opposite seat. He regarded her coldly as she recovered her breath.

'Was that your first accusation of theft?'

She coloured and bit her lip.

'You slipped away early. Our business was unfinished.'

She lowered her eyes. 'I thought it finished very successfully, sir.'

His eyes narrowed. 'For you, perhaps. Strip.'

She stared. '*What?*'

A muscle moved in his jaw. 'You heard, Madame.' He rapped on the roof with his cane. 'Drive on.'

As the coach jolted into movement Lucilla glared at him. 'You'd take your pleasure *again*, sir? This is an outrage –'

He leaned forward, eyes blazing. '*Strip*. Or I'll do it for you. You're wet and you're shivering. You might catch cold, then a fever. I'll not have a corpse on my hands.'

He leaned back with a slow smile. 'Besides, I'll enjoy the view.'

She pressed her lips together. He was a wonderful lover. Such passion, such energy – and only a few short hours ago. *How quickly things changed.*

She undressed slowly. He watched, impassive, his eyes lingering on her skin, drinking in every detail. As she peeled off her second stocking he leaned forward.

'Kneel.'

'*Now?*' She darted an involuntary glance at his trouser flap and then looked away. 'You would have me –'

He laughed softly. 'Relax, that was not my intention.'

With a swift movement he shook out a tasselled rug folded on the seat next to him and draped it around her shoulders. 'But the idea has distinct appeal. Later, perhaps. Now come here.'

In a swift movement he gathered her into his lap, holding her close with one arm. With his other hand he pushed a stray tendril of wet hair away from her face. 'A governess at Chatsworth, a lady-in-waiting at Windsor. Where next – Newgate? Dammit, Lucilla, when can I make you my duchess? We fuck in every bed in England except mine. Why do you hide from me? Do you doubt my love for you? I've no reason to doubt yours – I taste it whenever we meet.'

She buried her face in his neck and drank in the glorious scent of his skin. 'It's for your own good, sir. How can I marry you? I'm not your equal.'

He touched his lips to her forehead, his tenderness sending a tremor through her. 'You're intelligent, cultured. You've a brain the equal of any man's.'

Tears stung behind her eyes. 'I meant your *social* equal. I'm a widow with nothing to offer. The Earl's gaming debts –'

'We've been through this. Your husband's debts are a trifle. I've offered time and again to settle.'

'But people would say you'd married a gold-digger.'

With an impatient sigh he pushed her upright. 'You'd have me marry a *thief*? You're everything I need. And I want you in my own bed, not in other people's.'

With an impatient thrust he pushed her off his lap and rapped again on the roof of the coach. Once more it juddered to a halt.

'This ends now. I should make you pleasure me on your knees, or take you over mine and give you a sound spanking – or possibly both. You owe me the one and you certainly deserve the other.'

With a violent thrust of his boot he kicked open the door. It yawned open, revealing a patch of sticky, muddy track and a thick, dripping thorn bush.

She shrank back.

'Will you marry me, Lucilla? Yes or no? If you refuse

you can get out now and damned well walk.' His eyes glittered. 'And I keep the rug.'

Her stomach clenched. She'd never seen him so angry.

Had she gone too far? It tore her heart to do this; she loved him so. He'd pursued her for months, and he felt so good ...

Briefly she closed her eyes. 'Yes, then. But on one condition.'

His face darkened. 'Name it.'

She crept back onto his lap, wound her arms around his neck and whispered softly into his ear.

His arms stole around her as a slow smile spread over his face. 'The spanking *first*? Done.'

He captured her mouth, and for a long time held her locked in an embrace that filled her with heat, with longing and finally with relief.

* * *

As the sun came out, the coachman shrugged off his oilskins and grinned. From the slaps and squeals below he guessed the Duke and his lady were enjoying themselves. For once his spell out here in the rain might earn him a nice fat tip.

He jiggled the harness to spur on the team. The inn beckoned and so did its ale.

As the greys picked up their pace the giggles slowly died away and were followed by a pause. It ended with a loud male groan and a long, contented silence.

Christmas Carol
Heather Towne

'Please, sir, can you spare something for a poor, hungry woman on this Christmas Eve?'

The man stopped on the sidewalk and looked down at the woman huddled up in her coat in the alleyway. The snow was coming down heavily in London town, the temperature plummeting with the fall of darkness. 'I can give you nothing, madam,' he replied coldly, bundling his muffler tighter about his neck. 'On this eve or any other.'

Carol Christian smiled shyly in the gloom, then lifted her skirts to reveal a slender, well-turned ankle. The creamy-white smooth skin glowed in the night.

The man's dark eyes widened, and he licked his lips. 'Weelll ...'

Carol lifted the other side of her skirts and put that foot forward, revealing another young, slim, shapely ankle that gleamed up at the man.

His eyes flicked back and forth along the snow-encrusted sidewalk. There were still some shoppers about, store windows lit up with festive displays of toys and goodies and geese. The man touched the brim of his top hat and said, 'You can come along home with me, if you like. I may have something for you there.'

'At least we'll warm up, eh?' Carol responded, grinning shrewdly.

* * *

She knew all about Lord Pickwuzzit from her time as a scullery maid at the Fitzgully household, where she'd befriended the charwoman who had once scrubbed Pickwuzzit's floors, until the woman had made off with his bed curtains one haunting night. Martin Pickwuzzit was a tall, hard-featured man of forty and five years, director of a mercantile business that had prospered mightily with the opening up of trade overseas. He lived an outwardly frugal life in a two-storey stone side-by-side on Grub Street, all by himself. He'd had a partner once, and a wife, but they were both gone. It was rumoured that the man kept a fortune in gold in his humble abode. It was also widely rumoured that his one and only vice, to go along with no discernible virtues, was that he regularly enjoyed ladies of the evening.

Carol hurried to follow after him as he strode resolutely

through the thickening snow, elbowing his way past singing street urchins and stepping over blind men's dogs. He didn't slacken his pace until he reached the door of 227, and then he drew a large brass key out of his waistcoat pocket and inserted it into the lock.

He glanced briefly but intently for a moment at the rather ornate door knocker before turning the key and opening the heavy wooden portal. Carol stepped lively to follow after him, out of the cold gloom of the night and into the cool gloom of the house. Martin slammed the door behind them and locked it.

'What say we shed some light on the subject, eh?' Carol remarked, trailing Martin into the darkened living room.

He grunted, struck a match and lit the single candle standing on the mantelpiece.

'And a fire, sir?' she asked politely. Then, when the man grumbled but did nothing more, added, 'You'll be able to see me that much better, sir. It'll do my body good to be nice and warm.'

He glanced at her, then bent down and picked up a tin coal scuttle, dropped a few fragments of coal into the fireplace and lit them. A dim glow shed but a little heat and light on the room. 'Now, let's see the merchandise.'

Carol grimaced at the calculating thrust of the comment. But she began to slowly disrobe, stripping off her coat and bodice and skirt and petticoats and corset and pantaloons and stockings and shoes. And while

159

Martin stared transfixed at what she was doing, her own sapphire-blue eyes darted about the room, searching for anything that looked valuable, or looked like it might hide something golden.

A few minutes later, she was stark naked, her clothing strewn about her bare feet. Martin's eyes blazed with excitement. Hers were dulled with disappointment. 'Think I'll be worth your while, sir?' she enquired listlessly, having discovered nothing but the sheer dreariness of the sparsely furnished room.

Martin regarded Carol's lush body, her pink-cheeked, pretty face and rounded shoulders and full breasts and narrow waist and flared hips, her shapely legs that culminated at the apex in a triangle of dark fur that hid her sex. His trousers bulged with approval, his tall brow beaded with moisture. 'You'll do,' he stated bluntly.

Carol smiled. She cupped her breasts, hefting the pale, blue-veined masses and fingering the pointing pink tips, and spread her legs to more fully reveal her sex. Her curvaceous body shone in the candle- and firelight.

'I'm convinced. You don't have to make a show of it,' Martin commented dryly.

The smile trembled to stay upright on Carol's plush cherry lips, anger flashing in her eyes. She walked towards the man, jiggling in all the right places and in all the right ways that make a male's blood boil like pudding singing in the copper.

And despite her repugnance at Martin's brusque, businesslike manner, and his reputation, she had to admire his brutally handsome face and striking eyes, the thick, curly black hair that covered his well-shaped head. So that despite the coolness of the room and his attitude, her loins warmed and moistened and her nipples distended. And the sight of the huge, hard cock he pulled out of his unbuttoned trousers made her just a little weak in the knees.

She strolled up to him and grasped his tremendous erection. The thing pulsed with heat and power in her soft, warm hand, a slight flush spreading over the man's high cheeks. 'How do you fancy it, sir?' she breathed in his face, stroking his cock.

'Our transaction shall be a mutual, though limited, partnership. For I'm hungry, as well as aroused.'

She didn't understand the meaning of his words – until he suddenly dropped onto the threadbare carpet before the fireplace, on his back, and pulled her down on top of him, faces to genitals, in the rather risqué sixty-nine position. Carol yelped when she felt his cold, strong fingers dig into the ripe flesh of her buttocks; then she screamed when his hot, wet tongue speared through her downy fur and pouted petals and into her pussy proper.

'My, but you *are* the hungry one!' she exclaimed, the man licking urgently at her slit, bathing her pussy

161

up and down with his taste buds and saliva, his hard-lapping tongue.

She gripped and lifted his mighty erection, stuck out her glistening red tongue and swirled it around his meaty hood. He tremored beneath her, betraying his emotion. His tongue jumped onto her clit and teased even more engorgement out of the already blossomed bud. Meanwhile she poured her lips over his cockhead and sank her head down, consuming almost three-quarters of the pulsating pole in her wanton wet mouth.

But it was she that moaned again, her pleasured voice vibrating all along his cock, as he knifed his entire long, bladed tongue into her pussy and writhed it around, thrusting it back and forth. The man ate her out, his appetite not exaggerated, sucking and chewing on her flaps, penetrating and pumping her to the sexual core, mouthing her swollen hard button. She sucked on his cock with equal vigour, just to keep up.

It was no easy task – his cock bulging her cheeks and bumping up against the back of her throat – but it was a pleasant one, made all the more joyous by the man lapping at her pussy again, hard-stroking her slit with a voracious passion that flattened her fur to her flaps. She bobbed her head up and down, her lips sealed tight to the thick shaft, mouth pulling right up to the bloated cap and then biting in and plunging back down again. Here was meat enough for any half-starved woman, to be sure.

Then Carol suddenly halted in her sucking, her teeth sinking into Martin's cock halfway down. Because she suddenly felt Martin shift backwards beneath her, felt the man's strong tongue surge between her buttocks to stroke her bum crack sure and sound. She shuddered, surprised and even further delighted by the man's wanton appetite.

His fingers spread her cheeks and his tongue glided up and down between. Carol quivered with delight, her smooth, sensitive bum cleft shimmering with the stroke of Martin's bold tongue, the man fanning fire in her backside like he'd already done in her frontside with his bawdy licker.

She'd never had her butt cleavage so lapped before. The sensations were strange yet exquisite. She slid her lips off Martin's cock and tilted her head up, her mouth hanging open, basking in the breathtakingly intimate ass petting.

She knew she had to reciprocate – just as dirtily. She knew she had to, and she knew she wanted to. So she dropped his slickened cock, grabbed his hairy sack, darted her head forward and down and swallowed Martin's balls in one lusty gulp.

He quivered, his cock smacking her in the chin, his tongue lodging between her cheeks. Carol mouthed the man's testicles around in her maw, pleased with her action and his reaction, pleasured by the feel of the great nuts in her mouth. She hollowed out her cheeks and flared her nostrils, sucking on the sperm-laden pouch, eliciting a grunt against her wettened crack, a tongue rimming round her rosebud.

Martin was swirling the wet, flexible tip of his tongue around and around her tiny pink pucker, erotically answering back for her ball-basting. Carol closed her eyes, her bum and body buzzing with the wicked sensations, her tongue juggling the meaty marbles in her mouth. And then her eyes burst open, as Martin's hands pulled her buttocks far apart, blooming her rosebud, and his ruddy licker actually penetrated her anus to a head-spinning depth of two inches or more.

She almost choked on his sack, rotating her bum on that warm, writhing pink snake inside her ass. It only lasted a half-minute or so, but it was worth every second.

Martin's tongue evacuated her chute almost as quickly as it had entered, leaving glistening gape behind. Carol disgorged his balls, grabbed his cock again and sucked on the surging length as he lapped her sodden pussy once more, both of them realising that release was all but imminent.

The candle had burned down not a tenth of an inch and the coals were still red when Carol quivered and gasped amidst her ardent cocksucking, Martin's manly bum and muff-work bringing orgasm brimming to her sensitised pussy. She scraped his shaft with her teeth, bobbing her head wildly, body and brain shimmering with sensual delight. She hardly felt his slight buck, the spurt of hot salty semen against the back of her throat. She shuddered and swallowed with sheer joy, the street lady and business lord united as one.

For all of the man's legendary thriftiness, he gave generously of ecstasy, as good as he got.

Martin tossed a half-crown at Carol as she was dressing and handed her a frozen joint of mutton. 'Something to feed your purse and your stomach,' he said. Then he ushered her to the front door of his house and opened it.

'Oh, my, I've got a run in my stocking!' she said, lifting her skirts like the first time.

He looked down, and she clubbed him over the head with the mutton.

* * *

'I couldn't get nothing out of him. Well, information, I mean. Couldn't even get a good look around the place. He was all business.'

'Aye,' Bill Chizzlewick grunted, glancing suspiciously up at Carol, as he dragged the unconscious body of Martin Pickwuzzit down the hallway and into the living room. He left it to lie on the carpet in front of the fireplace.

The big man straightened and brushed snow off his broad shoulders. 'Too busy to do much poking around, I bet. Well, now that I'm in, I'll just have to ransack the place. I'll find his gold, you can be sure of that. I've got a nose for it.' He picked up the candlestick and swatted Carol on the bum as he walked by. 'Didn't I find you then, girl?'

As her confederate tumbled the house, Carol sat in the one comfortable chair in the living room watching Martin repose on the floor. She'd hoped to spend the night and pump the man thoroughly for his hiding place, or find it on her own while he slept. That way, she could've cut Bill out of his share of the loot he'd done nothing to earn other than put her up to it. But she'd had to change plans and take action when Martin had concluded his 'business' with her so quickly, and bring Bill into the picture.

She heard the big clumsy man curse upstairs, and something thump upon the floor. What a way to spend Christmas, she thought, folding her hands in her lap and sighing.

Soon, Carol was furtively rubbing her pussy with one hand, fondling a breast with the other, reliving the brief but intense interlude with the now unconscious man on the floor. She was just getting good and warm again, full of Christmas cheer, when Bill stormed down the stairs and into the living room.

'Damn it all anyway! I can't find a bloody thing worth so much as a farthing in this dreary lot!' he bellowed, stomping across the carpet and kicking at Martin.

Carol's hands flew off her intimates and she jumped to her feet. 'Maybe he doesn't actually have any gold.'

'Him, with a thriving business for so many years!? Come off it!' Bill kicked Martin again, and the man stirred. 'I'll just have to get him to spill his secret the hard-knuckled way, I will.' He clenched his thick fingers into two huge fists, as Martin's eyes blinked open.

'All right, you,' Bill snarled, dragging the dazed man up off the floor by his lapels. 'Time to spin old Bill a yarn made of golden thread. Otherwise, you won't have the brains left to count up to –'

Carol thudded the mutton joint against the back of Bill's head. The man dropped like a poleaxed ox.

She helped Martin to his feet and assisted him in dusting off his well-used clothing. 'The big brute attacked you when I opened the front door. He claimed you had some gold hidden hereabout in your home. Made me stay quiet as he ransacked the place.' She fluttered her long lashes, blue eyes glittering with brine.

'Mmm. I thank you, I'm sure,' Martin replied. Then he bent down, rolled Bill over, hooked his hands under the snoring man's beefy arms and dragged him out to the front door.

Carol opened the door for him, and Martin dumped Bill back into the snow-drifted gutter whence he'd come. 'You shall be rewarded for your good deed,' Martin commented wryly to Carol.

The reward consisted of a hunk of stale bread, a chunk of hard cheese and a glass of rum punch. Carol consumed all three voraciously, gazing across the rickety dining-room table at Martin and forcing a smile onto her lips.

'And now, dessert,' the man announced, taking Carol's hand and pulling her to her feet.

He led her up the creaking stairs, along a chilly corridor, into his slumber chamber. This room was as spartan as the rest of the house; the bed, when he whisked back the green bed curtains, small, lumpy and iron-framed. Martin rapidly disrobed, and Carol quickly followed suit.

She stared briefly at the man's naked body. Wiry muscles stood out on his arms and legs, his waist trim, chest matted with dark curly hair like his head and groin. His skin was pale and unblemished, luminescent, like hers, nipples just as pink. She reached out to touch his chest, bury her fingers in the whorls of hair, but he roughly pushed her down on the bed and mounted her.

Such a man wasn't given to cooing and coddling, or fondling beforehand, Carol reflected ruefully, feeling him spear his cock into her pussy. He was a hard man, his erection now fully re-formed as it stuffed inside her and sank all the way home.

'Yes!' Carol murmured, revelling in the overfull sensation. She grabbed Martin's curly head and brought his full red lips mashing down upon hers, kissing him, darting her tongue into his mouth.

His large hands found her large breasts and mauled them, as his pumping hips sent his cock churning within her, stretching and stoking her. She moaned into his face, twirled her tongue around his, hooked her legs around his waist and dug her heels into his clenching buttocks.

He shoved her breasts up and his head down and mouthed first one of Carol's stiffened nipples, then the other. Ardently if awkwardly, he kissed, licked and sucked her jutting, buzzing breast-tips, pistoning her cunt with his cock. She twisted her head about on the flimsy pillow, her dark hair flying, breath coming in gasps, feeling the man's mouth and hands and cock with her very being.

The bed violently creaked, the iron bedstead grating against the wall. Martin's buttocks clenched faster and faster under Carol's spurring heels, his cock pounding into her pussy. He slammed her heaving tits together and bit into both of her rubbery nipples at once.

Then, abruptly, he pulled back out. 'You won't deny me some rear-door pleasure as well, will you?' he gasped in Carol's face.

She stared at the man, uncertain exactly what he desired. He quickly showed her in no uncertain terms, digging his fingers into a tin of grease that stood on the bare wooden bedstand, then slathering his cock with the concoction, plunging his slickened digits in between Carol's buttocks and scrubbing. She jumped and yelped, the grease cool, the bloated hood of Martin's cock squishing up against her bum pucker hot.

She had neither voice nor time to protest. Martin's huge cap burst through her ring and bulged her anus, followed breathtakingly quickly by inches and inches and inches of the man's hardened shaft. Carol's eyes almost popped out of her head with the fearsome anal pressure, her pretty face flushing red. There was so much, stuffing her in a sexhole unused to stuffing. Martin was stretching her like never before.

He grasped and sucked on her breasts again, pumping his hips and cock just as vigorously as earlier, only up her ass now rather than her pussy. Carol clung to his neck with her arms and to his waist with her legs, rocking to the thrusting beat of his dong in her bung. She felt like she'd split right open, right down the crackline, the powerful plugging sounding deep in her soul. It was wickedly weird, unwholesomely wanton, yet really and truly wonderful once she got used to it.

Carol's bum and pussy and body burned. She clutched Martin's curls and dug her heels into his thumping buttocks, urging him to drill her violated anus harder and faster. But the awesome pressure and intensity were obviously even more onerous for him than for her, and he couldn't maintain them long. He had to abruptly pull out of the vice-tight, oven-hot pink tunnel of her bum and plow back into the silken pink sleeve of her pussy.

He hardly missed a stroke, thrusting into Carol's sex again at a furious pace with his battering-ram cock. She was dizzied, dazzled by it all, the searing of her chute, the sudden shift from back to front. They pounded together at a fever pitch, both primed for raucous explosion.

Carol screamed and buried Martin's face between her breasts, orgasm welling up and crashing through her body in waves. He capped those waves with white, grunting and jerking, dousing Carol's womb with heated sperm. As the clock struck midnight, the pair of them were partaking of that special Christmas spirit.

She tried to snuggle in his arms afterwards, but he rolled away from her and onto his feet. 'I'm afraid I have to ask you to leave. I'm expecting some visitors. A thank-you get-together.'

'But-but I can give you so much more,' Carol pleaded, rolling onto her side and displaying her body in a most lascivious manner. 'And-and maybe you can give a poor, beautiful woman who came to your aid – made you come twice – some small portion of that gold you keep hidden about your house.'

She'd come out and said it, no other option available to her now. She lowered her eyes demurely, hiding the burning gleam of lust for flesh and metal.

A smile flickered briefly across Martin's lips. 'I have no gold. That's merely an outdated rumour.' He paused, noting the disbelief in Carol's eyes. 'You see, I used to worship a golden idol once – the money idol. But then something happened to me about this time a year ago, something that profoundly changed my outlook on life. Since then, I've given all of my excess money to charity, to help those truly in need. That's why I live so frugally now.'

Carol's body sagged with disappointment, as she saw that the man was telling the truth. 'But I'm in need. I –'

'I've already helped *you* out,' Martin interrupted. 'By not calling on the police.'

He gripped her elbow and lifted her off the bed. He let her dress before escorting her down the stairs and to the front door, and out into the snowy night. 'A Merry Christmas to you, Carol. You're a very resourceful woman. I'm sure you'll have no trouble providing for yourself without my further assistance.'

She was about to protest one final time, when the door slammed shut in her face with a resounding thump. It was like the sound of a cold joint of mutton hitting someone on the head.